An Unveiled Secret

By

Alisa White

 New Generation Publishing

Chapter One

Gwyn cringed when a bell rang out as she opened the café door. She looked around the crowd while closing the door behind her. Melissa stood up and waved an arm to attract her attention. She blushed brightly, and her embarrassment kept her eyes firmly fixed upon the floor. She felt self-conscious as she made her way across to Melissa. She gladly sat down and hoped she could now melt into the background.

"It's so good to see you again," Melissa greeted. "I've got you a coffee. I guess you must've been back for nearly three weeks now. Tell me what Boston's like. What do you think of it?"

Gwyn was still flushed with embarrassment as she smiled shyly.

"It's chic, elegant and sophisticated, just like Lance's mum says it is, or at least the parts we saw are. It's hot and humid too. I'm still trying to take in that Lance doesn't know his way around."

"How can he not know his way around his home town?" Melissa laughed in disbelief.

Gwyn hesitated. Lance had confessed to having only been allowed to travel from their apartment to the office and back. Blake hadn't let him socialise. He didn't know anyone outside of work, and he had never been allowed to chat idly with the workforce.

"His dad bought him a car when he passed his test," Gwyn informed, "but he was only allowed to drive between their apartment and their country house."

"That's awful. You can't move over there if your lives are going to be like that."

Gwyn and Lance both knew they didn't want to do that. They had explored the city together, thanks to Nancy refusing to let Lance work while on honeymoon. She had insisted neither of them worked, and then she had held a garden party at their country house. She had introduced Gwyn to a host of stylish and well-groomed women, women who she had met again at the official opening of Nancy's shop.

"She wanted me there to mark the occasion," Gwyn explained, "and she introduced me to as many customers as possible. It sounds awful, but it was all so tacky. All the staff were dressed in old-fashioned dresses. Lance's mum told everyone they were like the ones worn by the women who lived in Arthur's court. They were nothing like the dresses of the period though. I couldn't say anything, and thankfully they were only worn on that one day. There were so many people there. The shop was packed all day."

Lance hadn't been with her all the time. The chosen day for the shop's grand opening had been no accident. The lawyers had called for a DNA test to prove Lance hadn't fathered Cindy's daughter, and Nancy had opened her shop on the day the samples were collected. She had wanted to distract Gwyn from what was happening, and it had worked up to a point.

Cindy had continued to insist that Lance was responsible for fathering her daughter. The Petersons hadn't read the out-of-court settlement statement thoroughly. Cindy had made her claim, and Blake had taken her to court as soon as the baby had been born. Blake had taken Lance along to give his sample, and Gwyn was glad of Nancy's distraction to keep her mind occupied while Lance was away. She had relaxed when he returned.

Gwyn stared at her mug of coffee.

"His dad actually stayed for a few minutes before going back to his office. The test came back negative, which was a real relief. It proves Cindy's been lying all along. Lance's dad gloated for days, especially when he hit the Petersons for the hefty fine that was included in the settlement if Cindy continued to accuse Lance. I was so glad when we flew back."

"And I'm glad you're back," Melissa stated. "Have you decided where you're going to settle yet? Are you staying here, or are you moving to America?"

Gwyn shook her head.

"We haven't decided yet. Lance's dad is expecting us to move over there. Everything's a mess there though, with his mum leaving his dad. She's bought and moved into the apartment above the shop in Newbury Street, and she's filed for a divorce. She's accused his dad of adultery and said she couldn't live with him any longer. He hasn't denied it. He's apparently had a whole load of affairs right through their marriage. We don't want to take sides. We'll get our own place if we have to move over there."

Gwyn smiled sadly. She felt as though they were caught up between two feuding adults. She wasn't used to two people fighting. Her parents had never fought. They had always been happy. She was glad to escape back here and start thinking about everything she would need to do if they moved to America. It was a welcome distraction, though the fighting was only making her want to stay here. They had a year before Blake expected them to return to Boston, and that year was going to pass far too quickly.

Chapter Two

Gwyn stood in the kitchen with her dressing gown wrapped around her. It was white in colour and almost reached the floor, despite the fabric belt tied around her waist. She was bare-footed with the summer being unusually hot, and living here in the city was doing nothing to ease the oppressive heat.

She had been preparing a salad when Lance had arrived home from work early. The music playing in the living room had drowned out the noise of him letting himself in. She had jumped when he had slid his arms around her waist. She had then smiled and relaxed again when she looked round and recognised him. She had been in his thoughts all day, and he had jumped at the chance to finish early. He had joined her at home, and he had refused to settle until he had led her into their bedroom.

The CD had finished playing by the time she got up and pulled on her dressing gown. Lance stayed where he was as she finished preparing dinner. He watched her leave the room then sighed as he stared up at the ceiling. Her dressing gown reminded him of the dresses and cloak she used to wear. They symbolised a special time of days gone by when knights were brave and chivalrous.

Gwyn soon returned with two plates. She handed one to him and sat beside him again. She knew he wanted her to take off her dressing gown and slip underneath the duvet with him. She was starting to feel fat and self-conscious though. She wanted to remain covered up so she could hide the weight she had gained. Her mind was distracted by her thoughts as she picked at her salad, and she hated the thought that she was about to change the relaxed atmosphere. She knew she needed to tell him what was on her mind though.

"Lance, we should be deciding where we're going to live. We agreed it's to be a joint decision, but I feel I'm being expected to make it for us. I can't do that. I'd like to know what you think. What would you say if I told you I don't want to live in Boston?"

"It wouldn't bother me. There's not much I'd miss."

"And if I told you I don't want to live here in England?"

He didn't answer for a few moments. She had caught him by surprise, and he wanted to think carefully about his answer. He put his plate on the floor and looked back at her.

"I'd miss some things but not others," he said. "Maybe we should do as mom suggested. Maybe we should buy a house here and in Boston. I know it'll be expensive, but at least we'll have our own home in both places. We'll not need to rely on my parents then. We could always sell one of them if we decide to stay in the other place."

Gwyn was still unsure. It sounded very extravagant.

"We can afford to do it thanks to the compensation my father's got for me from the Petersons. Why don't you go to the real estate agents in the morning and see what's on offer."

She still didn't look convinced. He tugged her dressing gown and kissed her exposed shoulder while he gazed fondly at her.

"Do you want me to be honest with you? I don't think I'll feel comfortable living in Boston with the Petersons there. They've somehow managed to keep what they'd planned to do quiet, so they've still got a lot of influence over a lot of people. I think I'd rather live here among people who've accepted me for who I really am."

Gwyn relaxed a little. She had sensed a tense atmosphere when they were in Boston, despite Nancy's best efforts to distract her. The people of Boston only knew the marriage of Lance and Cindy had been called off. Blake had disputed her claim that Lance had fathered her child and, despite the test results, Lance was being labelled the villain. He was now finally admitting he didn't want to return to Boston.

"I didn't say anything sooner because I didn't want you to give up the chance of starting a new life just because I'm not comfortable over there," he added.

"Do you honestly think I'd be happy living somewhere when you're not?" Gwyn asked. "I've seen how modern, stylish and sophisticated Boston is, and I'm not denying it. But this is supposed to be a joint decision, and I'd rather be surrounded by people who love and respect us and live in a slum than be surrounded by hostility while living in a palace. What you've said hasn't actually influenced me. It's just confirmed what I was already thinking."

He stared at her then made her jump as he took her plate and put it beside his on the floor. He then turned and started to kiss her. Maybe they should have had this conversation when they arrived back. It didn't seem to matter now though. She had seen that the new life she had once planned would have never worked out. They could both see it.

Lance stopped in the kitchen doorway and watched Gwyn for a few moments. He was facing the harsh reality of a new day. He was wearing the suit he hated and knew he was going to be separated from her while at the office all day. He was being forced to wait until the working day was over before he saw her again.

Gwyn was washing up the breakfast dishes in the sink. She always washed the dishes in the sink instead of using the dishwasher. She preferred it. She couldn't trust the dishwasher to do the job properly. Lance smiled fondly as he slipped his arms around her waist and kissed her neck. She turned and smiled before kissing him back. Her hair was pinned back, and wisps hung carelessly and partially covered an otherwise exposed neck. The scent of her perfume filled the air, making him ache for her all the more.

"You will go to the real estate agents today won't you?"

"Of course I will," she confirmed. "I said I would."

They had continued to talk yesterday, and their decision was now as good as made. They were now relieved they had dared to confess how they really felt to each other. They were determined to keep that confession between just the two of them. There was no need for anyone else to know just yet.

They only needed to believe they were buying houses both here and in Boston.

Gwyn sensed his reluctance to leave. Graham would be waiting for him though, and she wouldn't be able to get to the estate agents if he didn't go. He was delaying her with his reluctance to go to work. She kissed him one last time then listened out for him leaving. He was gone and leaving her free to run her errand.

She tidied the already tidy living room and made their bed. She picked up the discarded clothes from the floor and pushed them into the washing machine. She was ready to leave. She picked up her door key and took the lift to the ground floor.

The morning sunshine felt warm as she headed towards the centre of Bristol. The heat was already becoming oppressive and stifling, and the crowds of people that bustled along the pavements was something she still wasn't used to. She was glad they had chosen to stay here instead of moving to Boston. She would never be able to adjust to city life, no matter where in the world that city was. She belonged on the hills and in the open countryside, where the air was clear and pure.

She called at several estate agents before she found a house she wanted to view. She made the arrangements to look over the property and left the agent. She would tell Lance when he returned home and then they would view the property tomorrow. The decision over whether to buy would then be a joint decision. She was glad to have something definite as she headed back to the apartment.

She took the lift when she reached the apartment block and headed along the corridor to their door. She let herself inside and shut the door behind her before she turned. Her stomach then churned as her heart leapt up her throat. Someone was heading towards her and made her cry out in fright.

"Lance! I didn't expect to find you here."

Her stomach tightened again. He looked both pale and upset.

"I had a call at the office," he explained. "They called here, but they got no answer. I have to go back to America."

"But why? You can't go back, Lance, not after everything you said yesterday."

"I have no choice. I have to go back, and this time I'm leaving you behind. I'm sorry, but you're not going with me. I'm returning alone."

Chapter Three

Gwyn was dazed as she perched on the edge of the settee and looked round when the doorbell rang. She hesitated before getting up. She hoped Lance had decided to stay here, and yet she knew he would let himself in if he had returned.

Melissa stood in the corridor. She didn't need to ask Gwyn how she was feeling. She only needed to look at her expression to know. She was distraught about being abandoned. Melissa stepped into the apartment and quickly closed the door behind her. She then guided Gwyn back into the living room, made some coffee and put the mugs on the table. She glanced at the latest embroidery then focused on the sheets of paper gathered from the estate agents this morning.

"Have you decided to live here after all?" she asked.

Gwyn looked up at her.

"We decided to do what Lance's mum suggested. I'd arranged for us to go and have a look at one tomorrow morning. I didn't expect to find Lance here when I got back, and I certainly didn't expect him to…"

Melissa could hold back no longer.

"What's going on, Gwyn? Why has he suddenly flown back to Boston and left you here? He dotes on you so much, and he seemed so incredibly happy and relaxed here with you."

A tear rolled down Gwyn's face.

"It's Cindy Peterson," she explained. "She's accused Lance of exchanging his sample with someone else's so it looks as though he's not the father of her baby. Lance's father has insisted another sample be taken under strict security. He'd already booked Lance's flight. He had no choice but to go. He insisted I stay here. He said it won't do me any good keep on flying backwards and forwards, especially for this sort of thing. He's only trying to protect me."

Melissa hugged her.

"Of course he is. You don't need all that stress. You're much better off staying here and being well away from the publicity this is bound to attract."

Melissa felt angry with both Cindy and Blake. They weren't considering how others were being affected in their desire to vanquish the other. They were both proud, and both hated losing. She believed Blake was going too far this time. He really knew how to make a big spectacle out of any event, and he was being totally inconsiderate in his desire to prove his point in such a public manner. Gwyn really didn't need this right now. Melissa decided to change the subject.

"You are still going to look at that house tomorrow morning aren't you?"

"Lance insisted I do. He's asked Graham to take me over."

"I'll take you. I'll call Rick and tell him I want the car tomorrow. He can tell Graham he's not needed. Which house is it?"

Gwyn shuffled through the papers then picked one up. She hesitated when drawn to this single sheet of paper then snapped out of her trance and handed it over. She was glad she had at least had the opportunity to talk to Lance yesterday. She was glad, and relieved even, that they decided to act upon Nancy's suggestion. It just made sense for them to look for a house here while they were here. Gwyn sipped her coffee.

"Lance trusts my judgement, but I'll really appreciate having you with me. The stupid thing is he'll be back by the weekend. I wanted to postpone going until next week, but he insisted I still go tomorrow. He fears losing it if it's just what we're looking for. How likely is it that we find the right house first time though?"

"It has been known to happen, so it is possible. You have to go and have a look if you're going to find out. I wonder what they mean by "in need of modernisation". I wonder how much work it really needs."

Gwyn said nothing. She felt calmer thanks to Melissa's support. Maybe it wasn't such a bad idea to go and look at this house. It would be a distraction that would keep her mind occupied for some of Lance's absence. Her mind was filled with his fears that Cindy would force him to leave her. He feared being forced to live with Cindy instead, despite knowing how irrational his fears were. Cindy could never force him to leave his beloved wife.

"I hope this won't push him over the edge," she said. "I'm scared it'll drive him mad. We were so happy until his father phoned this morning. What if he can't recover from this constant harassment? He only wanted Cindy to just leave him alone."

"I'm sure it'll all be over once and for all soon. I can't see this sample testing positive. In fact I'm sure Cindy knows who fathered her baby."

Gwyn forced a smile. They knew for certain Cindy knew the identity of her baby's father. Blake was confident the truth would be revealed soon. She and Lance only wanted this to be over with soon so he could return to her. Maybe then they could be left in peace so they could get on with their lives.

Gwyn and Melissa climbed out of the car and stared at the ivy-covered house before them. The air already felt warm, and the bright blue sky was cloudless. A light breeze rustled the leaves in the nearby trees. There was no respite just yet from the oppressive heat that had been with them for the last two weeks.

A representative from the estate agent was already waiting for them when they arrived. He was eager to show them around. He opened the front door and followed them inside. He guided them from room to room, and he answered their questions as they stirred up the dust as they walked. They could now see just how much work was needed before the house was deemed habitable.

They looked over the garden from an upstairs window. Long grass was matted with brambles within the confines of a natural stone garden wall, it hiding any plant that might struggle to grow beneath it. There was nothing much to see, so the group returned to the yard in front of the house. Gwyn wasn't interested in the two derelict outbuildings. She had turned her attention to the nearby trees.

Those trees formed a natural barrier between the house and the road. The wood covered almost fifteen acres. Gwyn stepped in among the trees and glanced round when Melissa joined her. The estate agent was staying by his car and leaving them to explore this wood in peace. Gwyn moved further in among the trees before she stopped again and stood in silence. She appeared to be in a trance as she heard familiar voices whispering to her on the breeze.

Melissa watched in silence. Gwyn seemed to be under some kind of spell. Melissa's mind raced. Gwyn then suddenly snapped back to real life. She glanced at Melissa then gazed about her again. This place was ideal. She and Lance were meant to live here. She couldn't risk losing it. She needed to act and find out how to buy this property.

"Gwyn, do you realise how much work needs doing just to make this place habitable? It'll cost a fortune."

"I'm well aware of how much work the house needs. We could stay in the apartment until it's ready. We're destined to live here, Melissa. Arthur and Guinevere are waiting for us to move in. I know Lance will agree with me when he gets back."

Melissa's doubts did nothing to dampen Gwyn's enthusiasm. She wasn't convinced by what Gwyn had just said. If this was what Gwyn wanted though… she led the way back out of the wood. The estate agent was quick to make a phone call. They could then only wait for an answer.

The peace was shattered by a ringing phone after long minutes had passed. Gwyn waited with bated breath while she listened to the brief conversation. The agent switched off his phone and looked at her.

"As far as the current owners are concerned, the house is yours," he told her.

Gwyn bit her bottom lip as she gazed at him before she looked across at the house again. She suddenly felt nervous and a little scared. She had just put in an offer to buy a house that needed completely renovating. What if Lance didn't like it? What if he said he didn't want to live here when he got back and saw it? She was vaguely aware of Melissa talking to the estate agent through the haze of doubt and trepidation that gripped her. Lance should be back by the weekend, and he would be able to see the solicitor with her next week.

She snapped back to reality. She felt daunted by what she had just done, but she also feared someone else snatching this away from them more. She suddenly needed reassuring the house really would be theirs. The agent smiled kindly.

"We're not selling many houses at the moment. Not many people are interested in such a remote location, and fewer have the funds needed to buy and renovate this house."

Gwyn gazed at the house again. The money needed wasn't a problem for them. She bit her lip again. She wanted to take it all in and remember every last detail. She eventually turned away and glanced at the wood as she headed over to Melissa's car. She believed she could see Arthur and Guinevere standing just inside the trees. If she did though, it was only a fleeting glance. This property wasn't actually theirs yet, so none of them could move in until the contracts were exchanged.

A warm glow spread through her as she smiled and climbed into the car. She then stared at the house as Melissa drove away until she could see it no more. She was frightened of the prospect of owning her own house, and yet she couldn't help but feel excited at the same time. She was sure Lance would agree with her decision. His return couldn't come quickly enough.

Chapter Four

Gwyn switched on the light as the gathering dusk darkened the room and tried to concentrate on her stitching. Her growing concerns made her mind drift though. She had tried phoning Lance on several occasions in an attempt to find out why he hadn't phoned her yet today, but his phone was switched off every time.

She couldn't understand why Blake had refused to let him fly back here to her. He had given his sample, so she could think of no reason to stop him from returning. She wished, more than anything else, he was back here with her again. They all knew how ludicrous Cindy's claim was. Gwyn was still left with a tiny nagging doubt that refused to go away though. She wished she had gone with Lance, but she couldn't blame him for wanting to protect her.

She suddenly heard the sound of a key being pushed into the lock of the front door. She froze for a few moments and then looked round. Her heart pounded as she put down her embroidery and warily made her way across to the living room doorway. Lance was standing in the hallway. He caught sight of her as he closed the door, and he stayed where he was as he turned and stared across at her. He looked pale and tired, and his eyes were full of sadness.

He dropped his bag and gathered her up in his arms when she hurried over to him. He held her tightly and didn't want to let her go. She hadn't expected him back before tomorrow. They were instead now clinging onto each other. He was back here with her, and that was all that mattered right now. He had returned to her and was holding her as though he never wanted to let her go. She actually felt his relief as he held her closely against him. He was back.

Gwyn eventually pulled back. She pressed her hands against his cheeks as she gazed into his eyes and kissed him.

"I'll get you something to eat," she said.

He snatched hold of her and refused to let her move away from him.

"I don't want anything to eat just yet. I just want you, Gwyn. I need you."

He gazed steadily at her as he took her hand. She held his gaze and said nothing. She wanted him as much as he wanted her. She wanted to feel his arms around her as he held her against him. She didn't object or resist as he led her along the hall and through their bedroom door.

Gwyn wrapped herself in her dressing gown and tied the belt as she fled from the room a little too quickly. She pulled what she needed out of the fridge then closed her eyes as she leant against the sink. She desperately tried to steady her nerves as she wondered what had happened to make Lance behave like some kind of animal just now.

She looked round when she heard him call out her name. He had pulled on some shorts and was now standing just inside the kitchen door. He couldn't venture any further. His nerves, insecurity and shame stopped him from doing so.

"Gwyn, I'm so sorry. I never meant to hurt you. I've no idea why I did what I did just now. I'd never deliberately do anything to hurt you. Please, can you forgive me?"

She looked away for a moment then looked back at him again. She knew something awful must have happened to make him treat her in such a brutal way, but she didn't know what. He had only ever been kind, gentle and considerate. She hesitated then offered her hand as she called him over. He too then hesitated before he crossed over to her. He wrapped his arms around her and closed his eyes tightly.

"I'm sorry. I'm so sorry. Please forgive me."

She pulled away from him and smiled sadly as she gazed into his eyes. She didn't believe there was anything she needed to forgive him for. He hadn't been himself when he had arrived back.

"You must be hungry," she said. "I'll make you a sandwich."

Lance watched her and nervously took the sandwich when she handed it to him. She smiled again and urged him to go back to bed. She watched him leave the room before she put everything back into the fridge. She then picked up a sheet of paper on her way through the living room and joined him again.

She shut the door and put the paper onto the bedside table. She then took off her dressing gown and slipped under the duvet beside him. He had almost finished his sandwich. He couldn't look at her as he began to apologise again. She kissed his shoulder and pressed her fingers against his lips.

"What happened when you were in Boston?" she asked. "You haven't told me how you got on."

Lance put his plate down on the floor and stared ahead of him.

"The appointment was sooner than I thought. I had mom and my father with me. Cindy, her daughter and I had our samples taken, and they were taken away under tight security for testing. My father insisted I stayed until the results came back. Cindy tested positive as the mom, but my sample came back negative again. Cindy started to object, but my father shut her up by calling in Phil Jameson and insisting he gave a sample. My father let me come back here then. He said I wasn't needed any more."

"So your father has called Cindy's bluff."

"She's convinced I set her up. I haven't heard all the names she called me as I left. Mom took me to the airport, and my father phoned me just after I'd landed here. Phil Jameson's sample is positive, and it sounds as though Cindy was really abusive then. She hated being caught out so publicly. Apparently the judge has ordered her to pay compensation for the time and inconvenience it's caused us and extra for the distress caused."

"So it's all over at last," Gwyn smiled. "She doesn't have a hold over you now. She can't force you to do anything. She can't take you away from me."

Lance couldn't bring himself to look at her. He couldn't believe she still wanted him after what he had just done to her. She kissed his shoulder again, and he finally plucked up the courage to look round and gaze at her.

"I don't deserve you," he said.

"You've been under a lot of stress lately. I feared this would push you over the edge. I have a feeling you came pretty close with the way it affected you. You're back here now though, and it's all behind us. There's nothing Cindy can possibly now do to you."

He looked away again and swallowed. He had wanted to retreat back here before everything was revealed in the newspapers. He knew the people of Boston would now know the results of all three tests. He could imagine them all discussing it right now, and he was certain they would be tearing into him. More than anything though, he knew the Petersons wouldn't tolerate what had just happened. They would be after his blood.

Gwyn gazed at him. She couldn't understand how the people of Boston could blame him when Cindy had shown how promiscuous she was. She was the one who had originally wanted him to return. It was as though she had planned to trap him. They didn't know what her motive was. Lance knew how easily she twisted things around so she appeared to be the victim, and it would make no difference that she was the one who had cheated on him. It wouldn't matter how much those test results proved that.

Gwyn stroked his arm and kissed his shoulder for a third time. She then turned and picked up the sheet of paper so she could change the subject. Lance looked blankly at her. His curiosity was roused though as he took the paper and began to study it.

"It's the house Melissa and I went to look at," she informed. "The one we were going to view. It's an old farmhouse. The couple who used to live there sold the farmland when they retired. Their children aren't interested in working it. He died a few years ago, and the children have had to put their mum into a care home because of her health issues. The house has been empty for months, and no one's interested in buying it. It needs gutting and rebuilding, and the garden's enormous and completely overgrown."

She hesitated. She suddenly felt nervous.

"There're a couple of outbuildings and a fifteen acre wood included with the property. Arthur and Guinevere met me there. They told me we're destined to live there. It's a chance for Avalon to return to that wood. My offer's been accepted. We only need to go to the solicitors and exchange contracts for it all to be ours."

Lance had looked round at her when she mentioned Arthur and Guinevere. She bit her lip and hoped he wouldn't be cross with what she had done. He gazed at her for a few excruciatingly long moments as he slowly took in what she had said.

"Avalon will come back?"

Gwyn nodded.

"Melissa didn't want me to buy it with all the work that needs doing. She doesn't understand though. She doesn't know what Avalon means to us. We'll not be able to move in until all the work's been done, but if you agree, it'll be ours within weeks."

He suddenly relaxed and smiled as he gazed at her. His concerns and worries melted away to nothing. Avalon was going to return to them once again. They only needed to buy this property. He dropped the paper, took hold of her and kissed her. Everything he had endured in Boston was dissolving away. No matter what Cindy might now say, she couldn't deny that Phil Jameson had fathered her child. She had no hold over him and no reason to bother him again. Why should he care what the people of Boston thought of him? He had no intention of going back there. They only needed to sign those contracts, and then there would be nothing to stop Avalon from returning.

Chapter Five

Lance stopped his car in front of the house. It was early in September and the roads were quieter now the schools were open after the long summer holidays. He had taken today off work so they could collect the house keys and drive straight over here. He still hadn't seen this house—their house. He just knew he could trust Gwyn's decision.

He climbed out of the car and stared at the house. It stood cold and silent as he gazed at it. He couldn't accuse Gwyn of not warning him about the state it was in. He now understood why she had written a long list of work that needed doing. He could now see exactly what she meant. White clouds reflected off cracked and broken windows, windows that, along with the doors and roof, would need replacing.

He was used to everything being new and perfect. He hadn't experienced anything that had needed to be completely renovated. He couldn't even imagine what was going to greet him. Gwyn headed over to the front door, where she waited impatiently for him to join her. He followed her, opened the door then stood back and waited for her to step inside.

Lance stopped beside her and looked about the hallway. The rooms were empty and the floorboards were covered in a thick layer of dust. Gwyn could see past the dereliction and dust. She could imagine how it would look once the renovation was complete. The yellowing and brittle walls would be replaced with fresh plaster and covered with warm-coloured wallpaper. The kitchen and two bathrooms would be fitted out with modern fixtures. They would have central heating installed and the plumbing and electrical wiring upgraded. The house would be warm, fresh and clean by the time they were finished.

They slowly moved through the house before eventually stopping at the window of one of the five bedrooms. They could gaze out to the nearby woodland from here. Gwyn bit her lip and hoped they could move in by Christmas. Lance looked at her and smiled at her ambitious desire. He couldn't tell her how worried he was about the cost of the work needed. She was excited and enthusiastic as she added to her list of work she wanted doing. He was stopped from voicing his concerns by the sound of an approaching car.

Gwyn hurried out of the room and left Lance looking out at the arriving car before he followed her. The builder had arrived to assess the work. Lance remained silent as he followed Gwyn and the builder around the house. None of them denied the amount of work needed to modernise the house, and it was going to take time. The builder, however, had his workforce idle in the current economic climate, a workforce that would be glad to have some work.

"I'll speak to the guys," he said. "As long as this weather holds, we should get the exterior work completed before it breaks. I'll see if we can get everything done before your little one arrives. When're you due to have him?"

Gwyn blushed.

"The sixteenth of December."

"We'll do our best. I'll give you a call when I've worked out an estimate."

Lance remained quiet as they watched the builder leave. He then stared at Gwyn's seemingly endless list. She smiled and squeezed his arm.

"I've checked the shop's accounts. There's more than enough in there to cover the cost of the renovation work and with the previous owners accepting a lower offer, you've got more of your money in reserve for any unexpected expenses."

His concerned expression melted away as he relaxed and smiled. He had forgotten about the shop. Everything suddenly didn't look as bad as he feared. He should have known that, in her usual practical way, Gwyn had everything organised and under control. She suddenly tugged on his arm.

She was keen to show him the wood. The wood—the place that had made her so determined to buy this property.

He readily followed her into the nearby trees. They were surrounded by a mixture of oak, ash and elm, and the canopy provided a welcome respite from the heatwave that stubbornly gripped the area. He gazed about him as they moved deeper into the wood before they eventually came to a stop. They weren't alone. Lance immediately recognised the two people now joining them.

Arthur and Guinevere looked happy and relieved. Their future was secure. The path was clear for them to return once again. Avalon would reveal itself once the builders were gone. They would be reunited. Gwyn and Lance would have their safe haven back to retreat to when they needed it. Lance at last understood Gwyn's enthusiasm. He could see she had made the right choice. They had to own this place.

Arthur and Guinevere faded back among the trees. Gwyn and Lance watched them go. They moved only when the king and his queen were no longer in sight. Lance looked back at the house when they emerged from the wood. He wanted another look around. He wanted to see it all again now he understood why Gwyn had been so keen. She smiled as she eagerly joined him. He could see it all in the same way Gwyn did this time.

They eventually ended up in one of the large bedrooms at the back of the house. Gwyn stood by the window and gazed outside. There was so much work that needed doing. She silently wondered if, maybe, she had made a mistake. She wanted all the work to be finished right now so they could move in. She wanted to move out of the Bristol apartment. She wanted to be living here, in the house they now called their own. She didn't like relying on someone else for the roof over their heads. She could picture this house in all its glory, yet it was distant and almost beyond their reach.

Lance stood behind her with his arms around her waist. She suddenly smiled and looked round at him, and he seized the opportunity to kiss her.

"Which room do you want as the nursery?"

"The next one I guess."

She leant back against him. His arms were around her as his hands slowly and gently stroked her belly. They both knew there was no guarantee they could move in before their baby was born. They could only hope the builders could finish their work in time. This was to be their first Christmas together, and hopefully they could celebrate it here. Lance smiled and gently squeezed her. They reluctantly left the house and headed back to Bristol. She was quick to answer the anticipated phone call, and she was even quicker to accept the builder's quote.

"They really must be short of work," she remarked. "The scaffolding's going up this week, and they're going to start work first thing on Monday."

Everything was moving incredibly quickly after waiting for what had felt like an eternity. It was going to be impossible for her to stay away while the work was in progress. She once again wished it was all over.

Gwyn headed home with her groceries in a couple of bags. She looked round and smiled when Melissa appeared beside her. She didn't object or resist when Melissa took one of her bags as she invited her back for a coffee. The shopping was put away and coffee was made when they were back in the apartment. Melissa put her mug on the coffee table and picked up a completed embroidery as she sat down.

"You've finished it," she said.

"Yes. Lance is taking me over to the shop on Saturday so Laura can start preparing kits. I can't believe how naïve I used to be. Life was so easy when mum and dad were alive. It was so easy when they just gave the materials I needed to make a picture. Gareth just carried that on. I didn't give the admin side a thought, especially as he told me it was really complicated. It was such a shock when I found out what was involved."

"You were only fourteen when your parents died, Gwyn. You had no reason to think about all of that. I'm sure they'd have taught you if they'd survived. I guess they didn't want to dampen your creativity by bogging you down with the background work. Gareth just gave you the materials you needed so he could work out the costs. He obviously wanted to ensure you didn't give any thought to that at all. He made sure you had everything you needed so you wouldn't start to question anything. You were still only a child after all."

"I should have thought about it though. I let Arthur and Guinevere distract me instead. I was so close to losing it all," Gwyn hesitated. "I saw Gareth the other day. He was waiting outside for me. He didn't say anything about me having Lance's child though. He's emigrating. He's moving to Thailand. I'm sure he was trying to get a reaction from me. I'm sure he wanted me to try stopping him. I haven't forgiven him yet for what he did though. He'll be very wealthy over there with the money he's plundered over the years. He'll not need to work again, which I'm sure will suit him. I've got plenty enough to think about without fretting over my brother. I know Lance is worried. We're both hoping the house will be ready before this baby is born. I don't fancy moving after its arrival."

Melissa put the embroidery down again.

"We'll have to keep our fingers crossed. There's something else though isn't there."

Gwyn looked away from her.

"Lance's mum has moved a man in with her. Apparently he's an old family friend. He was married for fifteen years before his wife died of cancer about three years ago. She wants to bring him over with her when she comes over when the baby's born."

She wasn't sure she would cope with that at Christmas, but she felt obliged to welcome them no matter what time of year it was. She was going to have enough to deal with already with her first baby to look after. There was no doubt that their first Christmas together was going to be very hectic indeed.

Chapter Six

Gwyn looked round and smiled when Lance joined her. She kissed him then continued to serve out dinner. She had been busy today. She had fetched three of her embroideries which he had convinced her to get framed. She had then spent hours on Lance's laptop. She had, from furniture to cutlery, bought everything they needed for the house. She now felt tired but satisfied as she put their plates on the table and joined Lance. She immediately sensed how tense he was, and she asked him what was wrong. He glanced at her.

"It's nothing really. Mom phoned a couple of hours ago. She's heard a rumour that my father and Cindy have been seen together. I phoned someone in Boston I trust, and he's confirmed that Cindy's been with my father in the office for the past week. I guess it'll only be a matter of time before they come over here…"

He stopped abruptly and looked across at her. His father owned this apartment. It would be natural for him and Cindy to stay here when they did eventually decide to come here.

"What if they come here before we can move into our house?" he asked.

"We'll just stay somewhere else until we can move in," Gwyn told him. "There's always the flat above the shop in Glastonbury. It's not ideal with how far you'll have to drive in for work though."

Lance snatched hold of her hand.

"We'll do it. I'm not going to leave you here alone, not with the very real possibility that my father and Cindy could turn up at any moment."

"What about work? I assume this is Cindy's latest attempt to get her hands on your father's company."

Lance stared at her. The realisation of what she was suggesting slowly sank in. He couldn't work for Cindy Peterson, not now he knew the depraved acts she had wanted to be performed on him. He looked dazed and numb as he took a few long moments to take in what Gwyn had said. She talked on when she got no answer.

"What about Rick? He's in as deeply as you are. Your father knows he gathered all the evidence he has against Cindy. Why don't you phone him and invite him over? It'll probably be too risky for you to talk at the office. Anyone could overhear you there. It'll be much safer for you to talk here."

He hesitated then stood up and made his way to the living room. He snatched up his mobile phone and dialled a number while he crossed to the window and stared outside.

Rick nervously looked up and down the corridor as he waited for the door to be opened. He quickly looked round and forced a smile when Lance let him into the apartment. He followed him to the living room and politely greeted Gwyn as he sat on the armchair. Lance was wearing jeans and a sweatshirt, and he now perched on the settee beside Gwyn.

"What's all this about?" Rick asked. "I assume it's to do with what your mum phoned you about earlier."

Lance nodded. He had been too stunned to take in what he was told earlier. He had told Gwyn, and only then did he start to realise how truly awful their situation was. It looked as though Cindy had changed tactics. It looked as though she had wormed her way into his father's affections. They could only assume she planned to get her hands on Blake's company directly from him. She would become their employer. She would be able to order them to do whatever she wanted them to do. It was only a matter of time before Blake and Cindy came here.

"She'll be able to do whatever she wants to us, Rick, and we shouldn't forget about the person who helped you gather all that evidence against her."

Rick stared at him then suddenly cursed under his breath. He had completely forgotten about Will. He couldn't deny that Lance was right. Will did need to be warned about these recent events.

"Can you remember what you suggested last year?" Lance asked. "You told me we could set up on our own if the worst thing happened. It looks as though our worst nightmare is coming true. I can't see any other way out for us, and that includes the other person who helped us. I can't leave him behind. Will you phone him and ask him to come over and see if he'll join us?"

He held his breath as he waited for an answer. Rick suddenly doubted they should give up the safety and security that their jobs gave them. He was acutely aware of the punishment they would receive if they did stay though. In reality, they had very few options available to them. He and Will could move to another company. Lance, however, didn't have that choice. He wouldn't be able to explain why he wanted to leave his father's company, and Blake's reputation would stop anyone from wanting anything to do with his son.

Rick stood up and crossed over to the window. His mind was made up. All of them were in far too deeply to not take this threat seriously. There was only one real way for all three of them to escape from Cindy's clutches. They couldn't leave Lance behind after discovering what Cindy had planned to do to him. They had to stick together, and this proposal meant they wouldn't need to explain their actions to anyone. They only needed to persuade Will to join them.

Lance sat beside Gwyn as they watched Rick usher Will into the living room. He looked nervous and embarrassed. He didn't know how Lance would greet him now he knew he was the one who had helped to expose Cindy. Lance had every reason to hate him for the part he had played. Will stopped just inside the door, his eyes upon Lance as he was greeted and offered a seat.

"Lance, I'm really sorry about what happened between Cindy and me…"

"Please, don't apologise," Lance interrupted. "I can't thank you enough if the truth be told. If you hadn't helped to rescue me from Cindy, I'd have never had this opportunity to be with Gwyn instead. I couldn't see a way of escaping from her and, as it turns out, what she'd planned to do to me. I've now got an opportunity to return the favour."

Will looked at Rick, who was sitting on the chair he had brought through from the kitchen. He didn't understand what was going on, and he was seeking an explanation.

"Cindy's hitched up with Lance's father," Rick informed. "It looks as though she's trying to inherit the company directly from him. She'll be our boss, and I can't imagine her forgetting what we did."

Will's eyes widened as he ran a hand over his hair. Cindy was going to be their boss? This was it, they were done for. He couldn't imagine her being the kind of person who would forget or forgive.

"The software programme you wanted to develop," Rick continued. "The one Lance developed for Gwyn and his mum is proving pretty popular. We're seriously thinking of setting up our own company, and we want you to join us."

Will stared blankly at him for a few moments before he turned to gaze at Lance instead.

"We really want you to join us, Will," Lance told him. "We're still working on the idea at the moment, so there's nothing definite. We do know we're not prepared to stay at my father's company. We've already drafted out our resignations. We're going to leave as soon as possible, and hopefully before my father and Cindy decide to come over and see us."

Will wasn't so sure. He had so many questions he wanted to ask. This was all so sudden. It gave him no time to consider his options.

"When do you plan to start?" he asked. "And where are you planning to base yourselves?"

"There's nothing to stop us from starting up while we're still working for Blake," Rick answered, "and Gwyn's offered to let us set up in one of the spare rooms in their house when it's ready. Lance is taking her to Glastonbury tomorrow. Blake owns this apartment. He wants to get her out of here before Blake and Cindy turn up. He doesn't want to leave her alone here. They'll move over to their house from there when it's ready."

"Please join us, Will," Lance blurted out. "After everything you've done to help me, I really don't want to leave you behind. I don't want Cindy doing to you what she'd planned to do to me. I don't want her to hurt you in revenge. I can't just leave you behind and abandon you."

"It'll be a chance for you to show Blake how wrong he was to not support you," Rick pointed out. "It's a chance to show both him and Cindy how successful we can be without them. We'll not be actually competing against them, so there's no reason for them to try to crush us. I know we seem to be taking one hell of a risk, but what other choice do we have?"

Will gazed at them then eventually took the sheet of paper offered to him. He read through the resignation statement printed on the paper then looked back at them again.

"Can I think about it?" he asked. "I'll need to discuss it with Anna. This'll affect her too. I can let you know in the morning what our decision is."

Lance nodded. He could understand why he wanted to discuss this with his girlfriend, despite being eager to have him with them from the very start. It was only fair they gave him the time he wanted. Whatever Will decided, Lance and Rick were going to hand in their resignations first thing tomorrow. They were going to have to wait until then to find out whether Will would join them or not.

Chapter Seven

Lance was glad he was driving along the shelter of the hills as squally rain fell. They weren't far from the house, and they would be there in a few more minutes. He soon turned off the road and onto the tarmac lane that led to the house. Rick's car was already parked in the yard. Lance and Gwyn were joined by the four occupants as they hurried up the garden path.

Lance quickly opened the door so they could all spill inside. They were sheltered from the wind and rain as they pulled their hoods from their heads while Lance closed the door again. The hall was dark, with the only natural light shining feebly through the interior doorways. They couldn't see each other very well in the gloom, so they moved into the reception room at the front of the house. Rick now introduced Lance and Gwyn to Anna. They greeted her politely before Lance spoke on.

"It's still a bit of a building site I'm afraid, though it's looking much better compared to this time last week."

Plaster hid the network of wires and pipes, while radiators were fitted and a single light bulb hung from the ceiling. This room only needed the layer of dust covering the floor swept away for the painting and wallpapering to begin. Gwyn's curiosity was roused as she gazed around the room. What did the rest of the house now look like? Things looked promising if this room was anything to go by.

Anna was also looking around the room. Will had explained everything that had happened. She understood why they wanted to start out on their own. She also believed they were taking a huge risk, especially when Rick unnervingly confirmed it was. None of them were prepared to stay where they were though. They were viewing this as a calculated risk, and one they believed they would regret if they didn't take it. More than anything, they were determined to show everyone they could succeed.

Lance opened the door at the far end of the reception room.

"We've decided to set up our temporary office in here," he informed, "just until we can set up a proper office in one of the outbuildings."

He stopped just inside the room on the other side of the door. Bags of plaster were stacked against a wall, and the wires and pipes were on show. No one said a word as they gazed at the mess in the room lit by a solitary light bulb. This was supposed to be only a temporary arrangement after all. They had really come to inspect the outbuildings and decide which one to convert into their office.

Rick remained quietly confident that they would succeed, despite all the misgivings. Lance and Will were, in the cold light of day, beginning to question what they had done. It was too late now though. Their resignations had been submitted. They had no choice but to continue with their plans.

The group braved the weather and hurried across to the outbuildings, where they sheltered as best they could as the builder arrived. Mr Walters joined them. He was curious to know what they wanted from him. Lance and Rick explained. Mr Walters then examined a wall as he began to discuss with the three men what it was they actually wanted.

The three women kept back out of the way and said nothing. Gwyn was soon drawn back over to the house again. She wanted to have a proper look around to see how much work was completed. Melissa was keen to join her and see for herself how different the house now looked. She dragged a reluctant Anna along with her as she followed Gwyn across the yard once more.

Gwyn looked about her as she wandered from room to room. The house might feel cold, but it looked very different compared to when the property had been bought. The walls were covered with plaster, while double-glazed windows stopped the draughts that had once whistled through the rooms. The two bathrooms were almost finished, and the kitchen was starting to look like a properly modern kitchen.

"It all looks so different," Melissa commented. "I'd love to see it when it's all done."

They stood at a window at the back of the house. An open hearth was framed by red bricks and an oak mantelpiece. It took pride of place along a wall in this room. They watched the rain being blown across the nearby hills beyond the garden wall. Gwyn and Lance had chosen this room as their living room, and the room in which they planned to spend most of their time. Gwyn smiled as she rested a hand on her swollen abdomen.

"So would I," she said. "It would've been nice to move in straight from Bristol, but we feared Lance's dad and Cindy throwing us out. Lance couldn't settle until we'd moved into the flat in Glastonbury."

Anna looked horrified.

"They wouldn't throw you out would they? He wouldn't do that to his own son surely."

"You've obviously not been working for the company long enough to know what Blake Brookes is like," Melissa smiled sadly. "And Cindy Peterson is even worse. I suppose Blake does actually own the Bristol apartment. There really is nothing to stop them throwing Gwyn and Lance out. I can understand why Lance insisted you made that temporary move, Gwyn. He only wants to protect you. He doesn't want you facing Blake and Cindy on your own."

"I know," Gwyn said. "We didn't really have a choice. At least we had my old flat to go to. It's not as though we've been made completely homeless."

She looked round and smiled when the four men joined them. Lance immediately crossed the room and slid an arm around her while kissing the side of her head. He was oblivious to how uncomfortable the others felt by his simple action. They quickly made their excuses and left the pair gazing out at the nearby hills. Gwyn felt safe and comfortable with his arm around her, and she did everything she could to resist the urge to grab a broom to sweep the dust out of the house.

"We are doing the right thing aren't we?" Lance suddenly asked. "Setting up our own company I mean. It's a massive gamble, and there'd be nothing to stop my father from crushing us before we can even get started."

"There's no real alternative. Your father does own that company. I know Rick and Will could easily move to another one, but you realistically don't have that choice. I'm glad you've all decided to stick together. No one ever got anywhere without taking the odd gamble every now and then. Who says you're going to fail anyway? If it doesn't work out, we'll still have this house and my income from the shop."

"No, Gwyn, that's not right," he objected. "I should be supporting you. I'm not going to let you keep me."

"What would Cindy do to you if you stayed at your father's company? What would she likely do to all three of you? You don't honestly believe I could just stand back and do nothing while she exacts her revenge and makes you really suffer do you? I couldn't do that, especially when it's totally unnecessary. I have faith in all of you. You just lack confidence in your own ability. This is your chance to show your father what you're really capable of achieving. He'll see you'll not only succeed, but you'll do very well. I'm certain of it."

He couldn't share her confidence. He did want to succeed, but his fears prevented him from feeling confident. Gwyn gazed at him.

"You mustn't doubt your ability," she told him. "You've never been given the freedom to prove yourself. It's time for you to break free from the oppression that's held you back all your life. Away from your father and Cindy and their overbearing and derogatory manner, I'm sure you'll exceed all expectations. I believe this is the opportunity all three of you need."

She took his hand and led him out of the room. They locked the house before she guided him over to the wood and moved in among the trees. Lance knew where she was taking him. He knew when and where she would stop. This was their sanctuary. This was the one place where everything made sense. He could think far more clearly here, and he had needed no encouragement when brought here to meet the two people now joining them. Arthur looked down at him.

"You are going to succeed, Lance," he assured. "All of you have the talent and ambition to prove your father wrong. You'll be bigger than him one day. You'll prove far more successful. It'll be a success no one will be able to deny. You're destined to do far better than anyone's wildest dreams can imagine. You only need to believe in your own ability and ignore all the remarks made against you. You need to keep your faith and hold onto that conviction. Never forget we're always here to support you when you start to waver. You can't possibly fail. There's nothing in the way to stop you from succeeding. What you're offering is the next big thing that no one can do without. Success is yours, and don't ever forget that. We shall ensure you don't fail."

Lance watched Arthur and Guinevere fade away before he gazed into space. He had their support, and Arthur had given him the resolve he needed. They really couldn't fail with his help. They had the mighty King Arthur on their side. He looked at Gwyn and forced a smile. It was time for them to head back to Glastonbury.

Chapter Eight

Lance walked into the kitchen and found Gwyn sat at the table with Melissa and Laura. Melissa was reluctant to leave, despite his arrival. She was too engrossed in their conversation to want to leave. Lance joined them, and the group drank their tea as they ignored the falling rain. The flat felt warm, and the inside of the window was steamed up with condensation from the pans boiling on the stove.

Gwyn and Lance had kept most of their belongings packed in boxes now scattered throughout the flat. They felt cramped and closed in as a result. They couldn't relax properly, not while they knew they would be moving again within the next few weeks. They didn't regret moving here though, despite their inability to settle. They were instead relieved and a little happier about not living in the Bristol apartment.

Blake and Cindy had still not been seen here in England. Lance had, however, heard plenty of rumours about them. They appeared content with staying in Boston for now, and that had given the three the chance to work out their resignations in peace. They had reluctantly agreed to stay on until Christmas, unless Blake and Cindy arrived before then. They weren't going to hesitate to leave immediately if the pair made an appearance.

Melissa was about to get up and make her excuses to leave when she noticed the strange expression on Gwyn's face. She had seen this expression before, when she and Gwyn had stood among the trees next to the farmhouse. Gwyn was now gazing at the stove. She appeared detached from everyone else and seemed to be listening to someone who wasn't here. She then suddenly got up and crossed over to the old hearth in which the stove stood.

Lance didn't react as he watched her. He had quickly learned not to intervene when she talked to the ghosts of people from the past. The person she spoke to was very real to her, despite no one else able to see anyone. He could see no one, and that suggested her visitor was someone he didn't know. He could sense another presence, but he knew this person was neither Arthur nor Guinevere. There was no doubting that there was someone else here.

"Where?" Gwyn suddenly asked.

She looked round at an imaginary person stood beside her while she ran her fingers over the bricks that surrounded the stove. She then quickly looked back at that brickwork and slid her fingers over it a little more. She suddenly stopped and prized a brick out of the fire surround. A metal plate was behind it. She pulled it away and peered through the small opening she had uncovered. She brushed aside the cobwebs stretched across the opening and reached into the black space beyond. She grasped hold of what was hidden from sight and pulled out a large, re-sealable plastic bag.

"What's this?" she questioned.

She wiped away the remnants of the cobwebs as she moved back over to the table. She then opened the bag and pulled out some sheets of folded paper. She began to tremble as she stared at the words and numbers written on them.

"That's your mum's handwriting," Laura stated.

Gwyn glanced at her, but preferred to stare at the paper as she unfolded the sheets. Laura smiled fondly when Gwyn handed the first sheet of paper to her.

"I guess mum's teasing me," Gwyn commented.

She took the sheet of paper back and gazed at it for a few moments before she put it down on the table. She then turned her attention to the next sheet of paper and gasped as she handed it to Laura.

"How could mum know? It's the house we're having renovated."

Melissa had been looking at the first sheet of paper when Gwyn gasped. She took the next sheet from Laura and stared at the jumbled mess of symbols, letters and numbers.

"How on earth can you see that?" she questioned. "How can you know it's your new house? And what's this on this other sheet of paper?"

Laura reached across and tried to point out the shapes in the symbols. What was clear to her and Gwyn though was just a complete muddle to Melissa. She couldn't make out the shape of the house or the outline of Gwyn wearing a simple coronet, no matter how hard she tried.

Gwyn stared at the third sheet of paper while Laura tried to show Melissa what they could see. She looked puzzled as she gazed into space for a while before eventually focusing on Laura.

"I don't know this place," she confessed. "I've never seen it before. I have no idea where it is."

Laura took the sheet of paper from her.

"It looks massive," she remarked.

"What does?" Melissa demanded.

"It's another house," Laura explained, "and a really big one by the looks of it. It looks very much like a stately home or a large estate. How strange that your mum should do two houses. I wonder what it means."

Gwyn wasn't listening. She instead stared at the fourth and final design. Her face had paled significantly. Laura was quick to notice as Melissa and Lance concentrated on the first three designs. She took the sheet of paper from Gwyn and studied the mass of symbols for a moment or two. She looked back up at Gwyn then they both looked at Lance. He immediately went cold while feeling uncomfortable and embarrassed.

"How could mum have possibly known?" Gwyn asked.

She sounded unnerved as she spoke, as though she was shocked by what she could see.

"She couldn't," Laura replied.

She couldn't understand how Gwyn's mother could have possibly known.

"She must have been guided," Gwyn decided. "It's a premonition. She foresaw it all. We're meant to be together, and we're meant to live in that house."

"What about this other house?" Laura reminded.

Lance couldn't keep quiet any longer.

"What's wrong? What is it?"

Gwyn and Laura looked at him and said nothing for a few moments.

"This last chart," Laura eventually informed. "It's you."

Lance took the sheet of paper and stared at the jumbled mess of symbols. He, like Melissa, could make nothing out. He didn't understand these charts. He couldn't see the picture until Gwyn brought it to life with her needle and thread. Gwyn and Laura were the only people here who could clearly see the picture hidden in these symbols.

"It's definitely you, Lance," Gwyn stated. "The only difference is your hair is longer in this picture. If you didn't have it cut, it'd be a perfect match. This is why Arthur and Guinevere were so excited when they first saw you."

Lance was too unnerved to believe them. He couldn't accept what they were telling him, not unless Gwyn stitched the picture charted by her mother. Laura gathered up the sheets of paper and hurried away with them. Melissa felt uncomfortable. She gave her excuses to leave and scuttled away, leaving Laura to return with the charts and photocopies she had printed. She too was now keen to leave and head home. Gwyn and Lance were left alone.

Gwyn watched her go as she carefully stored the precious sheets of paper back into the re-sealable plastic bag. Lance felt guilty. He knew he should be working on his new business venture. He was too easily distracted by Gwyn and her discovery. He felt he should have been stronger and eager to provide some input alongside Rick and Will.

Gwyn served out their dinner. She felt unsettled. She should feel at home in this flat where she had grown up. She instead, after discovering those hidden designs, was impatient to move into the house. The builders were finished and the house cleaned thoroughly so the decorators could move in. They were in the middle of painting the woodwork and hanging wallpaper. She itched for it all to be done so they could get carpets laid and furniture in place. She wanted to be able to finally move in. They were so close to that day, and frustration was quickly taking a hold.

"Who were you talking to just now?" Lance suddenly asked. "I assumed your mom told you where to look to find her secret designs."

She gazed at him for a few moments, and then realised how her actions must have looked.

"Yes mum was here. I'm sorry if I freaked you out."

Lance smiled kindly.

"You didn't freak me out at all. Melissa was a little though, but then she's not used to this kind of thing. I guessed who was here, and I think Laura must've done too. I'm sure Melissa will get over it and learn to accept this kind of thing happens."

Gwyn looked unsure as she bit her lip. Melissa would maybe need to get used to this happening, but not in this way. She should have been warned beforehand. She now remembered her meeting with Arthur and Guinevere when Melissa had been present. She had thought nothing of that meeting, and she had given no explanation for her behaviour. It had simply been normal for her. She found it easy to forget that very few people experienced what she did. They couldn't possibly understand what was happening.

"I'm sure Melissa will get used to it," Lance said. "I just assumed it was your mom's way of communicating with you. I guess she decided the time was right to reveal her secret and give you this one last gift."

Gwyn managed a smile as she gazed at him. She had already decided to stitch the last of her mother's four designs first. She would see his reaction when it was completed. Her resolve strengthened. She could now think of nothing but that design of Lance.

Chapter Nine

Gwyn climbed into the car then looked back at the building as Lance got in beside her. The shop looked so small and tatty. It was squashed on both sides by equally small and quirky shops. So much had happened here. It was full of memories that would always remain with her. Her memories weren't tatty. They were rich, happy and treasured.

She had spent the last few days cleaning the flat while Lance took their boxed belongings over to the house. The flat slowly became less cramped, and the pair could gradually move around more freely. The last of their possessions were now loaded into the car. Gwyn continued to stare at the shop as Lance joined the heavy Saturday morning traffic and began to drive away.

It was the beginning of December. A cold wind blew while an icy rain lashed the windscreen. Lance, Rick and Will were still working at Blake's company as they helped to finish one last order before Christmas. Blake and Cindy had still not made an appearance. The three were growing increasingly nervous as the days passed. Lance wasn't thinking of that work today though. Today he was driving away from Glastonbury and along the side of the hills to the farmhouse.

Gwyn gazed at the house from the shelter of the car. They were here. They were finally moving in. After weeks of waiting, everything had fallen into place. They now only needed to climb out of this car and cross over to that front door.

Lance opened the door and ushered her inside before he closed the door behind them. The walls were covered with wallpaper, the woodwork coated with a fresh layer of paint and carpets were laid on the floors. Their distinctive smells intermingled in a heady mixture throughout the house. They smiled as they took off their coats and hung them behind the front door. They were home. They were in their very own home, and there was a mountain of unpacking to do. Lance stopped Gwyn as she began to move away.

"You've done nothing but clean these last couple of days. You've already done far too much, and I bet you're tired. I want you to go upstairs and get in the bath while I make some coffee."

"But…"

"You should be resting, not just for your sake, but the baby's as well. The unpacking can wait. There's no hurry. We've all the time in the world to get everything just perfect. Go and get in the bath and I'll bring you a coffee up. I'm not going to let you do anything else today. There're two more weeks before the baby's due to be born, and then another week before Christmas. You don't have to get everything done today."

Gwyn hesitated a moment then reluctantly climbed the stairs and disappeared into one of the bedrooms at the back of the house. The bed was waiting to be made with the wrapped bedding sat quietly upon it. She stared at it, and she somehow managed to resist the temptation to make the bed. Lance had told her to get in the bath, and she couldn't deny feeling sweaty and dirty.

She pushed the plug into the plughole and poured bubble bath into the running water. She then moved back into the bedroom and pulled some clean clothes out of her case. She sank into the bath water, washed her hair and cleaned away the sweat and dirt from her skin. She then lay back and began to relax as a thick layer of bubbles covered her. Maybe Lance was right. Maybe there was no immediate hurry to get everything unpacked. The house was warm and dry, and it couldn't be taken away from them. They were here at last, and there was no need for them to return to the flat in Glastonbury.

Lance walked into the room and made her look round at him. He seemed surprised to still find her in the bath instead of making the bed. He put her mug down and perched on the toilet seat as he gazed down at her. She looked calmer and more relaxed while covered with bubbles. She smiled as she glanced at the bubbles then back at him again.

"You're going to have quite a journey to work now aren't you," she said.

"It's not as far as from Glastonbury, and it's only for a couple more weeks. I told you, it was worth it just to know you're safe."

She smiled again. They had lived on a knife-edge while living in the Bristol apartment and while Lance worked his notice. That had all come to an end now, giving them both the chance to relax. They only needed Blake and Cindy to stay away until after this last order was completed. It would be good for Lance to finish on a good note.

She sat up and picked up her mug with bubble-covered fingers. Lance watched her, his gaze daring her to get out of the bath just yet. She was happy to stay where she was for now though. She was in no hurry to move as she sipped on her coffee.

"Are you going to let me make the bed when I get out this bath?" she asked.

"I'll let you do that, but nothing else. I don't want to take you to hospital after just moving in."

She bit her lip as she gazed at him.

"It's kind of scary and exciting isn't it. We're actually living in our own home, and we're about to become parents."

Lance smiled. His mother and step-father were due to visit when the baby was born. With the way things were going, they would probably be here over Christmas too. He pulled an envelope out of his pocket.

"This was on the doormat when I came over earlier," he announced. "It's about my application for permission to live and work here indefinitely. It's been approved, so I guess I'll have to let mom know when she comes over."

Gwyn's steady gaze made him smile. Thanks to their marriage and his new company starting up, he had been granted permission to stay and work here for as long as he wanted. Gwyn smiled broadly. She climbed out of the bath, quickly dried herself and hugged and kissed him. No one could force him to leave and never come back now. He really was here to stay.

She sprayed on some perfume and dressed. She then left Lance in the bathroom as she moved into the bedroom and dried her hair. She felt clean, warm and dry. She was brushing her hair when Lance emerged from the bathroom. He had showered and dressed in clean clothes. He now watched as she started to make the bed. They then stood by the window with arms around each other as they stared out at the hills beyond their garden. Those hills were deserted, with no one insane enough to venture out in this weather.

They eventually made their way to the kitchen, where Lance put their new possessions away into drawers and cupboards while Gwyn cooked. He was determined to make sure she did no more work today, and he was ready to step in if she tried to. They were soon eating their meal. Lance then loaded the dishwasher and guided Gwyn through to the living room.

Gwyn sat on one of the two settees and gazed at the logs stacked on either side of the hearth. She was glad they decided to keep the fireplace, despite the room being warm enough to not need the fire lit. Some framed embroideries were stacked against a wall waiting to be hung. A large television was next to the fireplace, underneath which was a DVD player. Gwyn smiled and resisted the urge to rest her feet on the coffee table before her. Lance put an arm around her.

"What needs doing?" he dared to ask.

"Those DVDs and CDs need putting away. Those pictures need hanging, the bed in the guest bedroom needs making and the nursery needs sorting out. And then there're all our clothes that need unpacking and putting away…"

"I'll make us some coffee," he decided.

He quickly stood up and disappeared out of the room. Gwyn stayed where she was and smiled. Two small side tables were behind her. One of them had Lance's laptop on it. She heard him moving around the kitchen, and she looked round when he joined her again and put two mugs on the coffee table.

"Thank you," she said. "Are you going to let me work on my stitching?"

"Yes I'll let you sit here and do that. I'll put the DVDs away."

She watched him kneel on the floor and start unpacking the box of DVDs. She then fetched a small box from a corner of the room and pulled out her latest embroidery.

"I forgot to tell you," she confessed, "the latest pictures are ready to be picked up from the framers."

"I'll pick them up on Monday, and I'll leave three more at the same time. I want you to stay here and rest, and I'm not going to argue with you about that."

She gazed at him for a few moments then smiled again. She settled back and started her stitching. She would, in reality, be glad when everything was unpacked and put exactly where she wanted it. She would only then be able to truly relax and finally feel at home.

Chapter Ten

Gwyn was relieved to get back home. A strong wind blew a heavy rain across the yard. She knew it was inevitable they would get soaked, and the thought made her hesitate before she looked at Lance then round at the back seat of the car. He followed her gaze and smiled.

"I'll cover him with the blanket," he promised. "I'll keep him dry as best I can. You wait here while I get the door open."

He climbed out of the car. She unfastened her seat belt as she watched him open the back door and fumble with a small blanket. Their son slept while safely secured in his car seat, but his arms jerked when the blanket covered him. She could wait no longer. She climbed out of the car and followed Lance as he headed towards the house. She then cursed mildly under her breath when in the shelter of the house.

"Lance, I'm so sorry. I've left my bag in the car."

He stopped her from stepping back outside.

"You stay here. I'll fetch it. It is, after all, why I'm here instead of at work."

He put the car seat down and headed back outside again. Their baby son had been woken by the wind and rain, despite Lance's best efforts to keep him covered. Gwyn felt guilty about forcing him back out into the rain. She had only needed to pick up her one bag, but she hadn't done it. The baby was crying though. She picked him up and carried him through to the living room. They were home.

She hadn't realised she had gone into labour yesterday. The pain she had felt had been nothing like the pain she had anticipated. She had picked up the telephone to call Lance when she had eventually realised what was happening. She had then felt another contraction which delayed her making that call. Melissa had let herself into the house at that moment. She had immediately taken charge and driven her to hospital before she phoned Lance. It had all been over by the time he had arrived. She had been taking hold of their new-born son when he had been shown into the room.

She now stood by the living room window and gazed out at the hills. They were deserted, the wind and rain keeping people away. Cado was beginning to settle again as Lance appeared beside them. Gwyn looked horrified.

"I'm so sorry, you're soaked through! Go and have a shower and get yourself dry. It's my fault you're so wet, so it's only fair you go first."

She refused to argue with him. She instead insisted he showered before he did anything else. She would wait as a penance for her own thoughtlessness. Besides, she wasn't yet ready to relinquish her hold on their son. She watched as he reluctantly left the room then looked back down at her baby son again. The name she had chosen for him had taken the nurses by surprise. She had needed to repeat it several times before she eventually explained about it being an old Cornish name. They couldn't hide their thoughts. She had only needed to look at their expressions to know they didn't approve of her choice. Cado was the name she was giving her son though, no matter what anyone else thought.

She looked down at Cado and smiled fondly. She wasn't yet ready to hand him over to someone else to look after, not even Lance. Cado was the centre of her world at the moment. She believed no one else would care for him as well as she would. He was everything to her, and he looked perfect as he slept in her arms.

Her smiled faded a little as she reluctantly laid him in his pram in a quiet corner of the room. He moaned a little but continued to sleep as she tenderly covered him with a blanket. She then watched him, just to make sure he was actually sleeping. She didn't want to leave him for a moment. She wanted to remain by his side, ready to gather him up in an instant if he showed even the slightest sign of distress.

Lance suddenly appeared beside her. He was clean and dry and ready to take over from her so she could have a shower. She didn't move. She wanted to stay right here and continue her vigil. Lance's voice was barely louder than a whisper.

"Go on. We were late coming here because he wanted a feed. You heard what the nurses said. He isn't likely to wake up again for at least another couple of hours. You have plenty of time to shower and feel more comfortable. Go on, I'll be here to keep an eye on him."

They were home and on their own now. They had no nurse on hand to give them advice when they were unsure of what to do. No amount of book reading could prepare them for this. This was the real thing. They were back at home and alone with a defenceless human life to nurture and look after.

Gwyn reluctantly moved away slowly. She did want to wash off the clinical smell of the hospital. She had no choice but to trust Lance to watch over Cado for the precious minutes she was away. She hovered in the doorway then hurried upstairs and stepped into the shower. She soaped herself down and let the spray of water rinse away the suds. She felt fresh and clean again.

She dressed in jeans and an over-sized shirt after stepping back out of the shower and drying herself. Her hair was brushed and dried and she then hurried back downstairs. Lance made some coffee while she loaded the washing machine. They then moved back to the living room, where they stopped beside the pram and gazed down at Cado before reluctantly sitting on the settee.

Lance felt happy and relaxed with Gwyn leaning against him and his arm around her. He had found last night almost unbearable. He had been here all alone while she was in hospital with Cado. She was back at home again now though. She was back here with him, where she belonged. She eventually broke the silence.

"I'd better start getting dinner ready."

He stopped her from getting up.

"I'll do it," he said. "You're not supposed to be doing anything except look after Cado. I'm supposed to be here to do things like cooking dinner."

She smiled quietly and didn't argue.

"Did you phone your mum?" she asked.

"Yes I did. She and David are coming over on Monday. I didn't think they'd want to stay in the Bristol apartment. I invited them to stay here. I hope you don't mind."

"Of course I don't mind. I only need to make up the bed in the guest bedroom. I'm sure they'd much rather stay here. What about your father? Have you told him?"

"Mom said she'll call him."

Lance went quiet. He hoped his father would be far too pre-occupied with Cindy to be interested in them. If he was going to be honest, he didn't want his father to come over here. His father's presence would only stir up the bad memories of his own childhood. He was determined to ensure Cado didn't suffer in the same way.

Gwyn stood up as soon as Cado stirred and started to cry. She picked him up and carried him back to the settee. Lance watched as she unbuttoned her shirt and began to feed him. He then got up and left the room. He felt compelled to cook lunch while Gwyn fed Cado. They had four days together before he had to return to his father's offices. They had four days before his mother and step-father arrived. He didn't doubt there would be nothing but complete bedlam until after Christmas. He would be working here with Rick and Will then. He would never have to put on his hated suit again.

Lance smiled. His hair was already starting to look a little untidy after his decision to let it grow. He knew his father would be furious with him for not cropping it short and styling it in the way his father had always demanded. His father no longer had any control over him though. He would instead be here with Gwyn and Cado, and that was what his life should really be like.

Lance opened the front door and let Rick and Melissa step inside. He immediately directed Melissa to the living room and watched her hurry away as he closed the door and glanced at Rick.

"How's it going?" Rick asked. "All sleepless nights and feeling ignored eh?"

Lance shrugged his shoulders.

"It's not so bad. Cado feeds at around eleven then not again until around seven in the morning. And Gwyn does remember every now and then that I'm actually here too. It's as though she doesn't trust me to do anything. She just has to do absolutely everything herself."

Rick smiled knowingly as he patted Lance's shoulder.

"I know exactly what you mean. Melissa was just the same. Have we had any e-mails today?"

"I haven't looked yet. We had a couple of orders placed yesterday, and there's a query about the programme Will's developing. Do you want to go and look while I make some coffee?"

Rick was staring at the computer screen when Lance joined him. He took the mug offered to him.

"You're right, we need to check on how Will's getting on before we reply to this query. We've had some more orders placed too. Things are going far better than I'd dared to hope."

Lance sipped his coffee.

"Arthur said it would."

Rick looked at him sharply.

"Avalon's coming to the wood here. It's why Gwyn was so hell-bent on getting this place. I have to admit I agree with her completely. I doubted that setting up this company was the right thing to do, so she took me over to see Arthur and Guinevere. They said we've got the potential to be bigger than my father. We only need to have faith in what we're doing."

"That'd be something wouldn't it. It'd be really good to show your father and Cindy how successful you are when given the chance."

"I wouldn't be doing this without you and Will."

"That's the whole point, Lance. We're all helping each other."

Rick looked beyond him as Will entered the room.

"Hello, Will. How're you getting on with that programme? We've had a query, and some more orders."

"Really, already?"

"Lance has been told on good authority that we're going to be more successful than his father."

Will was leaning in front of the computer.

"Oh, by who?" he asked.

"King Arthur," Rick informed.

Will quickly looked round. Rick surely had to be joking. Rick looked at Lance and then back at Will during a short and uncomfortable silence.

"No it's not a joke, Will," Lance told him. "We're being deadly serious. Maybe it's time I introduced you and explained, though we can't let anyone and everyone know. Rick and I have experienced things that can't be explained. I think it's time for you to experience it too, and then you'll see that we simply can't fail. Our success is guaranteed. Arthur and Guinevere will make sure it is. We only need to believe."

Chapter Eleven

Lance and Rick were sitting in Blake's office. A weak winter sun shone through the window behind them. They were staring at the computer screen, and were both too engrossed in their work to notice the two people striding towards the office. Stiletto heels echoed noisily, but the pair didn't hear the warning it gave. They only looked up when the door was flung open, and they stared open-mouthed as Blake and Cindy joined them. Lance quickly gathered his senses. He stood up and grabbed his coat.

"The keys to your apartment are on the desk," he informed.

He refused to look at them and said nothing more. He instead pulled on his coat as he walked out of the office and made his way down the stairs. He had almost reached his car when Blake caught up with him.

"Where do you think you're going?" he demanded.

Blake pulled him round and forced him to look at him. There was no sign of Cindy. She thankfully appeared to have stayed in the office. Lance dared to stare steadily back at his father. King Arthur was here with him with his support and protection.

"I'm going home," he said.

"You're not going anywhere. What happened with Cindy was a mistake. It was a simple misunderstanding. She's explained everything to me. I'm the one she really wanted to be with. She agreed to see you so she could be close to me. I've done everything you needed for you, and because of your jealousy, you've now frozen me out. You haven't even had the decency to tell me I have a grandson."

"I don't want anything to do with Cindy or with you while you're with her. I can't trust her, and I never will. I can't even bring myself to be in the same room as either of you."

"Well you're just going to have to get used to it. We'll be here while you're working…"

"I don't work for you any longer, sir. I've already worked my resignation notice. I agreed to carry on until Christmas to help your staff out, unless you and Cindy turned up. Everyone here knows we'd walk immediately if you did."

Blake stared at him for a few long moments before looking round. Rick and Will were standing nearby. Both of them were watching Blake and Lance carefully. Blake suddenly snorted with disdain.

"I don't believe you. You're being ridiculous. I bet you haven't even got another job to go to. Who'd take you on? You'll just be a burden to your wife and show her how useless you really are."

The air grew cold as Blake spoke. The light darkened, and then everything reverted back to its usual state. Blake was the only one who didn't sense the threat made towards him. Lance, Rick and even Will felt the ominous foreboding in that threat. King Arthur was here. Rick broke the tense silence.

"We've set up our own company, sir. We answer to no one, except for ourselves. We're dealing in software so we pose no threat to you."

Blake laughed harshly.

"Then you're guaranteed to fail. I'll give you six months at most. You'll then be able to tell me what it's like to lose everything. Don't look to me to help you out though. You can beg as much as you want, there's no job here for any of you. I'll see you later, Lance, when I call in to look at my grandson. Hopefully he'll turn out to have more backbone to him than you have."

"You're not welcome in my home," Lance dared to tell him. "You're to stay away from me, my wife and my son."

Blake glared at him. He couldn't believe he had dared to speak to him in such a way. Lance continued to gaze steadily back at him. Blake's expression suddenly changed. He appeared to be unnerved as he chose to change the subject.

"Who said you could stop having your hair cut and styled in the appropriate manner?" he demanded.

"It's my choice, sir. I'm sure you want to get back to Cindy. We'll keep you no longer."

"You're completely wrong about her. She's got spirit and drive and ambition. You'd do best to stay here and learn from her."

Lance wasn't interested in listening to his father's claims, especially if they were about Cindy. He dared to turn away, climb into his car and drive away. He had made his escape and left Blake standing in the car park. He had, with King Arthur's support, emerged victorious over the tyrant who had raised him. He had escaped from his clutches, and he was at last free to live the life he wanted.

Gwyn held Cado as she looked out of the kitchen window. She had prepared the guest bedroom, so she now had nothing to do but wait. The plane should have landed about an hour ago, which meant Lance could arrive here at any moment. He hadn't wanted to return to his father's offices today. He had wanted to stay here, with her and Cado. He had agreed to go back though. He couldn't back out if he was going to be fair to everyone else. They weren't to blame for what had happened. They didn't know why he was leaving though. Rick and Will were the only other people who knew how vain Blake was now being for believing everything Cindy was telling him.

A car turned off the road and approached the house. Gwyn recognised it immediately. She flicked on the kettle, opened the front door and retreated back to the warmth of the kitchen. She was spooning coffee into four mugs when she heard voices in the hall. Nancy only needed to hear her calling out to head to the kitchen. She crossed the room and gazed at Cado. He was sleeping peacefully while resting against Gwyn.

"Oh look at him! Isn't he gorgeous," Nancy cooed. "How come you've given him such an unusual name?"

"It's the name of one of the knights," Gwyn informed.

"Oh I see."

Gwyn had heard Lance and his step-father climb the stairs. They left the cases in the guest bedroom and returned to the kitchen. Nancy was pouring boiling water into the four mugs so they could move through to the living room. Gwyn reluctantly laid Cado in his pram and covered him with the blanket. Nancy had immediately noticed the pictures hanging on the walls.

"Look, David, Gwyn's embroideries have been framed."

They examined them for a while before they sat on one of the two settees. Gwyn looked embarrassed and smiled quietly as she joined Lance on the other settee.

"It was Lance's idea. Are you going back to the office today?"

Lance shook his head. He wasn't going back to the office, not today or any other day.

"It's lucky you're staying here, mom."

Nancy gazed at him.

"Blake and Cindy have turned up haven't they."

"So Cado and I have you here at home with us for good," Gwyn said. "I'm glad, even though it's sooner than you'd hoped."

"Oh good," Nancy sounded pleased. "Can David and I borrow your car tomorrow? I'd like to catch up with Laura and then go shopping."

"Take the car if you want. I'm going to check our e-mails."

Gwyn gently took hold of his arm.

"Surely that can wait until tomorrow. Why don't you go and change out of that suit."

He hesitated then put his mug down and stood up. He wasn't gone for long. He quickly returned, dressed in jeans and a sweatshirt. He began to feel more comfortable and relaxed now he was home and dressed casually. Blake and Cindy couldn't touch them here. They were safe. There was nothing Cindy could do to hurt him.

Cado roused from his sleep as Lance walked back into the room. He dared to pick up his son and cradle him on his lap for a few minutes. Gwyn inevitably and eventually took him from Lance. She retreated to their bedroom so she could feed him in privacy. Lance was alone with his mother and stepfather. He suddenly felt nervous. David broke the awkward silence. Lance quickly looked across at him.

"You mom's told me about King Arthur. It sounds fascinating. I'm hoping you'll tell me more."

"Gwyn's the expert. You'll need to ask her."

David smiled as he stood up and moved to one of the pictures on the wall.

"She seems a very nice young lady. Are all these pictures her work?"

"That one is. Some are her mom's."

"She's very talented. It all looks very romantic. What must it have been like to have lived in those times?"

David looked back at Lance.

"I really am interested in hearing more about King Arthur. Your mom's told me he's come back in you."

Lance stared at him then looked at his mother.

"How can you tell anyone about that, mom?"

"It's OK, Lance, I promise I'll not tell anyone. It does make me wonder if you're the one who should tell me about the king though. I don't mean right now though. Maybe you'll do that at some time in the future, after we've got to know each other a little better."

Lance didn't answer. He felt nervous and wary with the way David watched and spoke to him. His behaviour wasn't normal. His behaviour was creepy. Lance doubted he actually did want to get to know him better, let alone discuss King Arthur with him. Nancy tried to change the subject. She suspected that Lance was recovering from his meeting with Blake and Cindy. She hoped they wouldn't visit them.

Lance didn't want to discuss his father. Blake had desperately tried to convince him that Cindy wasn't the evil person he believed her to be. Blake didn't understand what his life with Cindy had been like though. He wanted nothing more to do with her. Blake, as always, adamantly believed her knew best while refusing to listen to his son. That ensured Cindy's success in making an even bigger fool out of him. Lance wanted to shut them out of his mind and life. Blake had made his choice, and that choice made Lance turn his back on him and walk away.

Gwyn returned and offered Cado to Nancy to hold for a while. She eagerly took her grandson and left Gwyn struggling to resist the urge to snatch him back and settle him in his pram. She was at a loss at what to do and hesitated. She then headed to the kitchen and started to prepare dinner. Nancy soon joined her after she had let Lance take Cado from her.

"Perhaps we should check into a hotel. I feel as though we're intruding here."

"Nonsense, I won't hear of it. I know things are awkward between Lance and his step-father at the moment. They need to spend time together if they're going to get to know each properly though."

"David's a good man. He's nothing like Blake. I expect they've just got off to a bad start. Perhaps I shouldn't have told David about King Arthur coming back in, Gwyn. I don't think Lance is going to forgive me."

Gwyn promised to talk to him.

"I reckon David would've made a much better father than Blake," Nancy said. "I do hope Blake doesn't turn up here."

"I'll be surprised if he doesn't. I'm sure we'll manage when he does, especially as we'll have Rick and Will here with us during the day."

"I hope so, Gwyn. He's changed so much since he got involved with that Cindy Peterson. He was arrogant enough before. There's no talking to him now. He's refusing to listen. I'm so glad Lance got out when he did, and I really hope they'll be successful."

Gwyn smiled and decided to keep quiet. She wasn't ready to tell her that Arthur and Guinevere had assured them of their success. They were destined to do very well indeed. Arthur needed to ensure their success for his own survival. Nancy changed the subject, and Gwyn did nothing to return to Lance's predicted success. Some things were best left unsaid, and this was one of them.

Chapter Twelve

Lance watched Gwyn as she got up. Cado had been whimpering for a few minutes before he cried properly. She lifted him out of his crib while Lance checked the time. It wasn't quite seven o'clock in the morning. Gwyn sat on a chair by the window and began to feed her son. Lance watched her for a few minutes then got up and disappeared into their en-suite bathroom. He showered and dressed in his jeans and sweatshirt. He still found it strange, not putting on his suit. The last few days had felt strange.

Gwyn was covering herself up when he joined her in the bedroom again. She changed Cado's nappy then handed him over to Lance. It was her turn to shower and dress, and Lance kept hold of their son while she dried her hair. They were ready to make their way downstairs. Gwyn headed to the kitchen and began to cook breakfast. Lance meanwhile settled Cado in his pram and gazed down at him before he suddenly moved away and joined Gwyn in the kitchen.

Nancy and David had been out for most of the day the other day. They had eventually returned, and they had spent the evening decorating a large Christmas tree with lights, tinsel and baubles. Nancy had waited until the following day before she placed an array of brightly coloured parcels under the tree. Lance still felt uncomfortable with the number of parcels. It symbolised his mother's addiction to shopping, and her argument of having a new grandson only sounded weak.

Lance was getting along no better with his step-father. David was trying too hard to step into Blake's shoes, and Lance wasn't yet ready to accept him. He found David's eagerness to be accepted through appearing enthusiastic about King Arthur too unnerving and overbearing. He couldn't openly discuss Arthur with just anyone, and least of all with someone he didn't know very well. He needed time to accept and trust him, and David wasn't making it easy for him to do that with the way he watched him constantly.

There always seemed to be something that needed doing in the office. Lance was glad he could retreat there and spend his days with Rick and Will. The days passed all too quickly though, and he was still glad to be back with Gwyn and Cado despite Nancy and David also being here. Today was Thursday, and he didn't know how the last three days had passed so quickly.

Today passed just as quickly as the last two days. He now found himself sitting beside Gwyn in the living room. They had eaten dinner when Rick and Will had gone home, and they were now settled in the living room with Nancy and David. Gwyn was working on her stitching while Cado slept. She joined in with the conversation as she worked. Her picture was slowly forming beneath her fingers, and they could all start to see what that picture was.

The relaxed atmosphere was suddenly interrupted by a loud hammering on the front door. The conversation stopped abruptly. Lance then stood up and left the room. He could already sense who was standing on his doorstep. There was only one person who could hammer on his door with such force. Blake had discovered where they lived, and he was now calling in on them. His voice thundered out as soon as the door opened, leaving them all in no doubt of who their visitor was.

Blake stepped inside as soon as the door opened. His voice boomed out as he barged past Lance and headed towards the living room. Panic immediately rose inside Lance as he closed his door and hurried after his father. King Arthur was already by his side, and the king's presence calmed him. He could focus upon getting back to the living room to protect his wife and son.

He slipped past his father when Blake stopped just inside the living room doorway. He stared directly at Nancy and David, as though surprised to find them here. His mouth then set in a hard line.

"I might've known you two would be here," he remarked.

"What do you want, Blake?" Nancy asked.

"I want to speak to Lance. I don't doubt you've already poisoned him against me though."

Lance was acutely aware of Arthur standing beside him as he dared to speak. The king gave him a confidence he had never experienced before. He felt as though he could challenge and defeat anyone, no matter how mighty his foe might be.

"No one's mentioned you, sir. You're the last person I'd want to discuss."

"You don't mean that," Blake scoffed. "It was all just a silly mistake. Cindy would've never hurt you."

"That's not true, sir. I want nothing to do with her, or you while you're with her. We're not going back to work for you. I'm not going back. And we're not sorry we've left your company."

Blake continued to insist he was wrong. Lance remained uncharacteristically calm and resolute though as he refused to believe what his father said. Blake quickly grew increasingly agitated, and his raised voice inevitably woke Cado. Gwyn immediately got up and picked up her son. She held him close to her as she comforted him. Blake seemed to ignore her as his voice grew louder while he continued to force his opinion. Lance stood his ground. His unnatural defiance in his desire to protect his wife and son easily annoyed his own father. Blake's face turned red with rage and frustration until he suddenly snapped and turned on Gwyn.

"Can't you silence that child so we can hear ourselves and concentrate on what's important?" he demanded.

Lance's expression revealed the painful memories of his own childhood. He stared steadily and directly at his father as Arthur's courage coursed through him. He felt confident with the belief in his own ability to shield his family.

"You're to leave and not come back," he stated calmly. "This is my house. Gwyn is my wife, and Cado is my son. You're not welcome here. I want you out right now."

"Look, Cindy only wants those DVDs and memory sticks," Blake said, "the ones Rick had. She thinks he hasn't handed them all over."

"Does she really think I'd have something like that here? If Rick says he's handed them over, then that's what he's done. There's nothing here for you. It's time for you to leave and never come back."

Blake glared menacingly at him. He then suddenly threw his arms up in frustration and turned to leave the room.

"You're no son of mine," he claimed.

Lance dared to follow him out of the room. He stopped by his front door and watched his father climb into the company car. So this was what all of this was about. Cindy wanted all of the DVDs and memory sticks from them. He closed his front door and took a deep breath to steady his nerves. He then turned towards the living room. Gwyn had followed him. She stood nearby and smiled softly as Cado lay quietly in her arms. He had defended them, and she couldn't be more proud of him.

He wasn't going to stand by and do nothing while his father treated her and Cado in the same way he himself had been treated. He was now trembling, as though the enormity of what he had just done was beginning to sink in. Gwyn smiled a little more as she hugged him. She had seen the expression on Blake's face. He had appeared to realise what he had said, and he had momentarily come to his senses. The tough businessman had immediately returned though, and that moment had passed.

Lance willingly hugged her as he quickly regained his composure. He took Cado from her and carried his son back to the living room. Nancy and David were standing in the room. They both looked concerned as he entered the room again. He then hesitated before crossing to the settee and settled Cado on his lap. Gwyn wasn't with him. She had instead disappeared into the kitchen to make some coffee.

"Are you alright, Lance?" Nancy asked.

"Yes," he snapped.

He glanced at her then relaxed a little. His voice was softer when he spoke again.

"Yes, I'm fine."

David looked shocked.

"Has Blake always spoken to you like that?" he questioned.

"He speaks to everyone like that," Lance remarked in an off-handed manner.

"It's my fault," Nancy said. "I should've stood up to him. I should've made your life much easier for you."

"You can't change what's already happened, mom. We can only stop it from happening again."

"Maybe so, but what's going to happen when you return to Boston?"

Lance didn't answer straight away. He looked at his mother, and guilt showed on his face.

"We're not going back to Boston, mom. Everyone's too hostile towards me. We've decided to stay here. I'm sorry for deceiving you. I know I said we'd buy a house in Boston too, but we've decided to stay here. I've already been granted permission to live and work here. It's got nothing to do with my father and Cindy though. I submitted my application before he'd even got involved with her."

Gwyn walked into the room as he spoke. She put the tray onto the coffee table and sat beside him as Nancy began to object.

"But, Lance… oh, I suppose you're right. Things can be a little uncomfortable at times. And you're obviously happy here."

Lance smiled. He was happy here. He could wish for nothing more. It didn't mean they would never visit them though. They would do that. Nancy forced a smile.

"What's all this about Blake wanting some DVDs and memory sticks?" David suddenly asked.

"It's some evidence gathered against Cindy. It revealed her motives for wanting to marry Lance. She was only doing that so she could get her hands on Blake's company," Nancy said.

"No wonder Cindy wants them. It looks as though she's going to get his company after all though."

"She's welcome to it. I don't want it. I've never wanted it. I don't know how they're expecting us to hand over something we don't have though."

Lance surprised them all with his comments.

"Are you sure they have every last copy?" Gwyn questioned. "It's obvious why she wants them all. Whether she has them all or not, she'll never know for certain you don't have another copy hidden away somewhere."

Lance looked at her then stared into space. She was right when she suggested that Cindy would never know for certain if she did have every last copy. She would always have a nagging doubt eating away at her. She would never know if that evidence would come back to haunt her. Lance would always have this hold over her.

Everything suddenly became crystal clear. This was why Cindy was showing so much interest in Blake Brookes, and he was arrogant enough to believe her. She and her parents were getting what they wanted after all—everything except for one thing. Lance had escaped. He was no longer within her grasp. Cindy couldn't exact her revenge on him. She couldn't touch Rick or Will either. She would also always wonder whether they did have a copy of that evidence against her. She was being forced to leave them unharmed. Lance smiled as he realised that, for the first time in his life, he had the advantage.

Chapter Thirteen

Lance was glad when the weekend was over. David was trying far too hard to be friends, and he was far too interested in hearing about what Lance's life had been like in his father's shadow. Lance didn't want to talk about his life under Blake's rules. He wanted to forget about it, and he wanted to pretend it had never happened. Monday eventually dawned to the sound of falling rain outside. He retreated to the office and was opening the e-mails when first Will and then Rick joined him. Will was far from happy.

"You won't believe what that cow's done."

Lance kept his eyes upon the computer screen.

"Who?"

"Cindy Peterson. She's sacked Anna just because she's my girlfriend. Just before Christmas too. Would you believe she's claiming Anna could leak their business plans to us. How ridiculous is that? She's only an office junior for heaven's sake! She couldn't find anything out that we don't know already. How on earth could Anna be a threat to them?"

Lance had already looked round when Cindy was mentioned. He looked at Rick then took a deep breath as he looked back at Will again.

"She'll be looking for a job then, and I know who to go to for advice."

Will watched as he disappeared out of the room. Rick started to pull on his coat.

"You'd best put your coat back on," he said. "It looks as though it's time for you to meet King Arthur and his queen. Just to warn you though, Guinevere's easily mistaken for Gwyn."

Will gazed at him and reluctantly pulled on his coat. Lance was wearing his coat and trainers when he joined them again. They hurried across the yard to the shelter of the nearby wood. The trees provided a refuge from the rain, despite being devoid of leaves. The bare branches were knitted together above them, and the atmosphere was tranquil and quiet. Will hesitated then reluctantly followed as Lance headed away. He was wary and unsure as he sensed that something unnatural was about to happen. The trees stretched away in all directions as the wood seemed to have increased in size.

Lance stopped suddenly and abruptly. He ignored Rick and Will as they almost walked into him. They had reached the spot where he was heading to. There was nothing special about this spot. To Lance, however, this very spot was sacred. He didn't move as he gazed directly ahead of them. Will watched him for a moment or two. He then looked at Rick before he looked back at Lance again. He was about to ask what was going on, but he instead cursed under his breath while taking a step backwards. His eyes were wide with disbelief. Rick grabbed his arm to stop him from backing away any further.

Two ghostly figures were approaching them. One was tall, large and clad in chainmail. The other was beautiful and elegant. Will stared at the woman who now stood before them. She was dressed in a simple, full-length white robe, a silver belt tied around her slender waist while her light brown hair cascaded down her back.

Will couldn't understand how Gwyn could have changed and come over here in such a short length of time. He had seen her when he had arrived this morning. What was she doing here with another man? And where was Cado? How could Lance just accept his wife being with someone else? Will said nothing as Lance bowed his head as he greeted them.

"You're seeking the answer to a question."

Arthur's voice was surprisingly gentle. Lance nodded. Arthur and Guinevere would already know of Blake and Cindy's presence. Lance suspected they also knew of Anna's dismissal. Guinevere smiled in her usual warm manner, it captivating Will as he continued to stare at her. She gazed back at him for a few long moments before her eyes moved back to Lance.

"You'll need some extra help soon," she said, "and you should be awarding yourselves a proper wage. You'll soon recoup your losses in the New Year. What you have to offer will be in great demand, and Anna will be a great asset to you. You can trust her, and bringing her here to join you is right for you all."

Lance bowed his head again. He had already known what they should do. He wasn't ashamed of coming here to seek advice and reassurance though. Arthur spoke again.

"Your father will eventually realise and admit to the mistake he's making. That won't be until after he sees how successful you will become. You've done the right thing with everything you've all done."

He was staring directly at Rick, as though he knew of a guilty secret he was keeping. Rick looked away, and when he looked up again, Arthur and Guinevere had melted away.

"OK, I'm officially freaked out now," Will said.

Lance looked round at him.

"Why? You heard what they said. Anna's supposed to join us and help us out. Gwyn's too busy and Melissa's got her own job commitments. It'd save Anna having to look for another job, and I can't think of anyone else we can trust. You won't say anything about what's just happened though will you?"

"Do you really think I'd tell anyone about meeting King Arthur and Gwyn?"

Lance gazed blankly at him.

"That wasn't Gwyn. She's in the house with Cado. That was Guinevere, Arthur's wife."

"I did warn you," Rick reminded. "Shall we get back to the office so you can phone Anna?"

Will didn't believe that Anna would agree to join them. It would be highly risky. Lance started to lead the way back to the house.

"I hope you don't doubt what Arthur and Guinevere have just told us. You really do need to trust them. They can see things that we can't. And besides, what's the worst thing that could possibly happen?"

The worst thing that could happen was the business would fail and they would all lose everything they had. Lance was the one who had the most to lose. He had a new home, and a wife and new-born baby to support. He had put all his money into this venture. Rick's daughters were older, and he had almost paid off his mortgage. Will and Anna would lose their jobs and possibly their home. They could always move back in with their parents. They were taking a massive risk, yet Lance was convinced they would succeed. He believed completely in the two apparitions who had appeared before them just now. Will still wasn't convinced that Gwyn wasn't one of them.

Lance disappeared when back in the house so he could put away his coat and trainers and make them some coffee. Anna was predictably shying away from the offer. She believed it too risky for both her and Will to be employed by a new company. Will's doubts returned and convinced him that Anna would refuse to join them.

"Go fetch her," Lance urged. "Bring her here so she can discuss it with Gwyn."

Will still wasn't convinced, despite Lance's assurance that Gwyn wouldn't mind. Lance understood how hard it was for Will to believe what they had been told. Their orders, however, were an indication that they would succeed. Rick studied what was on the computer screen.

"Lance is right," he said, "we've had a whole load of orders placed over the weekend. Even if we hadn't gone over to see Arthur and Guinevere, these orders tell us we'll need to take on someone else soon. We can't deal with these orders and work on developing more software at the same time. I don't think we can afford to be distracted from developing the software. Perhaps Cindy Peterson has inadvertently done us a favour, and I'd much rather take on Anna than someone we don't know. At least she'll be earning a wage."

"OK, I'll go and fetch her," Will relented.

Lance watched him go. He was confident that Gwyn would convince Anna to join them. At least Nancy and David had gone out for the day. He could only let Gwyn know what they had been told to prepare her for Anna's hopeful appearance. There was nothing else they could do but wait while they tried to concentrate on work.

Will eventually returned with Anna. He couldn't believe how easily Gwyn convinced her to join them. It seemed like madness, and yet here she was sitting in the office with the three men. One person, she informed, had already walked away from Blake's company before she was forced out. She was sure that others would soon follow. It was as though Cindy was being deliberately obnoxious so she could purge the undesirable staff from the company.

"That wouldn't surprise me," Rick remarked. "Well, I guess we should draft out a contract for you. Maybe we should do the same for ourselves too. We've been too busy to give it a thought."

They weren't going to mention King Arthur and Guinevere to Anna just yet. It would only convince her they had gone mad if they did. Lance would know when the time was right to reveal all to her. Whatever Gwyn had said to Anna, it had convinced her to join them. She too would now be as determined as they were to show Blake and Cindy that they could, and would, succeed. They were going to prove them wrong.

Chapter Fourteen

Rain had been falling when the day dawned, and that rain turned to snow during the morning. The small group in the office constantly looked outside to keep an eye on the weather. Rick, Will and Anna were now beginning to wonder how much longer they should stay before they headed home. They had an increasing amount of work to do though, and all three wanted to carry on for as long as possible. It was too easy to become engrossed in their work. Will eventually glanced outside then quickly looked a second time.

"Damn! Look who's turned up."

The others looked out of the window and watched a familiar car roll to a stop in the yard. Lance stood up.

"I'll go."

He slipped out of the office and quickly walked through the reception room. He pulled on his coat and trainers then let himself outside. The other three hesitated before they moved into the reception room, where they heard Lance pull the front door shut behind him. Rick searched Gwyn out while Will and Anna stayed in the reception room. Gwyn was holding Cado when she joined them, and Nancy and David followed her. They looked outside and saw Lance standing by the garden gate as Blake climbed out of the car. Blake crossed over to Lance as Cindy joined them.

"We've come to tell you we're flying home. I'm leaving my company to Cindy. You're getting nothing from me."

Lance said nothing. He knew his silence would infuriate them far more than any other reaction. He was determined not to be surprised by anything they might say. King Arthur had joined him. He sensed the mighty warrior's presence alongside him as he provided his support and protection.

"We're getting married this summer," Cindy informed, "and your father's going to treat me right."

Lance raised his eyebrows as he glanced at the large ring on Cindy's finger when she flashed it at him. He hadn't expected this announcement. Maybe they could surprise him after all.

"We're making our union official, and we're definitely making sure Cindy inherits everything that's mine. She'll ensure it only grows bigger. She won't make a complete hash of things or destroy everything I've built up from nothing."

Blake was puffed up with his own importance. Lance dared to speak at last.

"That won't be easy with a small child to look after," he remarked.

"Oh don't be ridiculous, Lance!" Cindy scoffed. "I'm not caring for Melody. I've got a nanny doing that. I don't want my daughter pestering me and getting in the way. I don't suppose you can afford a nanny. That's lucky really, considering the ridiculous name you've come up with. I mean, Cado—what kind of name is that?"

The temperature immediately dropped considerably as the sky darkened. Blake and Cindy were unaware of the displeasure she had caused with her remark. Arthur was angered by her ignorance, and he wanted to punish her for her comment. Guinevere encouraged him to delay her punishment though. She believed the time to administer revenge hadn't come. Lance smiled quietly. The relevance of the name was very clear to those who understood.

"Is there anything else that's brought you here, or would you rather get to the airport?"

"Yes there is," Blake confirmed. "We wanted to give you the chance to admit to having another copy of the DVD and memory stick. You only need to hand them over."

"You already have all the copies," Lance insisted. "There's nothing for you here."

Blake stared condescendingly at him.

"No, there isn't anything for me here. You really are no son of mine. I have no son."

David was about to move so he could offer Lance some moral support when Anna yelped. She snatched Will's arm as David looked back out of the window. A shadowy figure had appeared beside Lance. This ghostly apparition towered above the trio as he seemed to shield Lance from his unwelcome visitors.

"What's going on?" David asked.

"It's King Arthur," Gwyn informed. "He's come to support Lance. Guinevere's here too. She's in the trees."

The group looked across to the nearby wood. How could King Arthur and Guinevere be here? It was too outrageous to believe, and yet here they were before their very eyes. Could it really be true, or were their eyes deceiving them? Gwyn continued on.

"Please don't be frightened, though I can understand your fears. We don't like to mention this until people have the chance to get used to the idea of this."

"But why are they here?" Anna asked.

"Arthur was trapped on Avalon while forced to wait for the person deemed worthy enough to come along," Gwyn explained. "Lance proved to be the one who possesses the qualities required. He demonstrated true courage and a true belief in the legend. He's earned Arthur's protection, and his assurance that he succeeds in anything he strives to do. If Arthur is to endure for many years to come, he needs to ensure Lance doesn't fail. No matter what anyone tries to do, he will be successful."

Anna stared at her in disbelief before she looked back out of the window again. Gwyn had spoken words of a madman, and yet there was no denying what they could see before them. The powerfully built, chainmail-clad apparition certainly appeared to be protecting the diminutive person beside him. The woman in the trees looked just like Gwyn. She was regal in her flowing white robe and the simple silver coronet upon her head. Gwyn, however, was standing here with them with Cado in her arms. How could this be possibly happening? Anna's head span. David was the one who spoke with a voice barely louder than a whisper.

"So it is true. King Arthur has come back."

Gwyn smiled. King Arthur had returned, and he was working through Lance. Her husband had the luxury of the great king's wisdom to call upon. He could seek Arthur's counsel whenever he needed it. They could achieve anything together, even the seemingly impossible. Guinevere had also returned. She lived on through Gwyn. She and Lance had been chosen to achieve the great things that Arthur and Guinevere wanted to achieve.

It was impossible not to believe Gwyn as they stared out at the imposing apparition standing beside Lance. Blake and Cindy were smirking as they now moved away from Lance. They were unaware of the presence of the once mighty warrior and his queen. Lance continued to stand his ground. He moved only when the car had disappeared down the driveway.

Lance stopped just inside the reception room doorway when he found the group staring at him. He now realised they had been watching him. He felt uncomfortable as he realised how much they had seen. He instinctively took Cado when he was handed to him, then Gwyn and Nancy left the room. They soon returned with some coffee, and the group sat on the selection of settees and chairs in the room. It was time for them to talk openly about what they had just witnessed.

Lance remained silent and let Gwyn explain. She could make sense out of the illogical. Lance was distracted by his thoughts as clear memories of his recent conversation filled his mind. Gwyn's explanation quickly came to an end. Nancy now wanted to know why Blake and Cindy had come here. Lance became the centre of attention again, and he hated every moment.

"They're flying home. Cindy's inheriting my father's company, and everything else he owns. They're getting married in the summer."

"What, well that's it then! Blake's lost his mind. I don't suppose he'll want that baby around though. Where is it anyway?"

"Back in Boston, and in the care of a nanny. They still think we have a copy of that DVD and memory stick."

"Worried are they? They should be."

Lance stared at Rick.

"You have got one haven't you," he accused.

"Of course we have. Did you really think we wouldn't keep a copy of something that important to us? I'm sorry, Lance. We didn't mean to deceive you. We didn't know if you'd be able to keep up the charade with your father…"

"Well he's not my father any longer. Don't forget I've been disowned."

Lance stood up and left the room. He should feel relieved about having finally escaped from his father's clutches. Blake's remark had cut like a knife though, and it left him feeling deeply wounded. He didn't want to remain with the others right now. He wanted to flee the room and return to the living room with Cado. He was frustrated, angry and upset. He hadn't wanted Blake's company, so why was he bothered about Cindy getting what she wanted after all?

Gwyn suddenly appeared beside him. He looked at her then back outside again. He had wanted to be on his own, but he was glad of her company. He readily agreed to pull on his coat and head over to the wood. He was going to Avalon so he could clear his head.

Chapter Fifteen

Lance covered Cado to protect him against the inclement weather then stepped back outside. He and Gwyn hurried over to the nearby wood and slowed when among the trees. They were shielded from the wind and snow in here. They hesitated for the briefest of moments before they continued on and stopped once again.

Avalon was due to eventually appear and take shape again at this spot. The lake and its island were just waiting for the builders to finish converting the outbuilding. They would then return to them. Gwyn and Lance both knew the reason behind the delay, and they could wait. They both knew in their hearts that it was already here despite it not being physically visible. They just needed to be patient for a while longer.

The pair sat down and Lance settled Cado on his lap. He ensured his son was still wrapped in the blanket before he gazed through the trees before him. Gwyn was sitting beside him, and she made him feel comfortable and perfectly at ease. She could always make him feel this way, right from their very first meeting. There was no pressure on him at all. If he didn't want to talk then she wouldn't force him to. They both knew, however, that he would inevitably do just that. It was as though he was unable to stop himself from blurting out what was on his mind. They sat here quietly, and he was acutely aware of her gently stroking his arm. They both knew it was all she needed to do to get him to talk.

"Why should I care, Gwyn?" he suddenly asked. "After the way my father's treated me, why does it bother me so much that he's disowned me? I really thought things were turning out alright. We'd got married and you were expecting Cado and Cindy was exposed as the fraud she is. How did she convince my father otherwise? How did she manage to take my father away from me? That's the only thing I feared happening—that she'd turn my own father against me."

"There's still time for your father to see her for what she really is. He could still realise what she's doing. She'll make a mistake sooner or later."

She sounded calm and quiet as she spoke. Lance couldn't see Cindy doing that again. She wouldn't be so easily fooled a second time.

"I wish my father would see she's only interested in getting her hands not only on his company, but also on all the evidence we had against her. Speaking of which, I still can't believe Rick could lie to me like that, even if it was probably for the best. I really wouldn't have been able to look at either of them in the eye if I'd known."

He suddenly glanced at her before he stared ahead of him again. The trees were stripped bare of leaves and their branches reached up into the featureless white sky. There appeared to be no life or anything of interest in here at all. They both knew better though. They were both waiting in anticipation for what was to come. Lance knew that, by believing Cindy really did have every last copy of that evidence, it was what had given him the resolve and conviction he had needed.

"It's why Guinevere looked at Rick in such a strange way the other day isn't it," he said suddenly "She knew he'd kept a copy back didn't she."

He could sense her smiling. Guinevere and Arthur had both known what Rick had done.

"I believe your father will come back to you. You only need a little faith. Maybe it'll happen when he sees how successful you'll be and how wrong he was to doubt your ability."

"That was Cindy really. She's the one who said we're guaranteed to fail. She always did put me down and tell me I'm no good at anything. She even…"

Lance stopped suddenly and refused to look at her. She gently stroked his arm as she urged him to continue.

"She had no right to say what she said. She had no right to cast aspersions on your integrity. I know you're nothing like her. I know you'd never see other men like she did—and still does. I should sue her for slander for suggesting that…"

Gwyn smiled quietly and continued to stroke his arm. He eventually looked round at her.

"You don't need to prove anything. I know you'll never cheat on me. I know I really am Cado's father. Cindy's just trying to stir up trouble between us."

He looked away again. There was a short silence before Gwyn spoke.

"Are you sure it really is your father disowning you that's upset you and not the suggestion Cindy's made?"

Her eyes were soft and kind as he looked at her again. She smiled as she carried on talking.

"Cindy made a mistake when she made such a suggestion here. To make that allegation about us is to make the same allegation against Arthur and Guinevere. That'll never be tolerated, and you know that as much as I do. Cindy has sealed her own fate by making that comment."

Lance gazed at her and suddenly smiled slightly as he relaxed a little.

"Don't let her win, Lance. Don't let her comments eat you up inside. Just bide your time and watch what happens instead of taking the bait. Sometimes you don't need to do anything to exact revenge. Just stand back and don't lower yourself to her level. You'll only have your father pitted against you if you retaliate now. Keep your dignity and just watch as she brings about her own downfall. It will come. Arthur and Guinevere will make sure it does, just like they'll ensure you'll prove to be a successful businessman without being hard and ruthless. It is possible to be successful while still being nice to people. You're destined to be respected far more than your father and Cindy."

"But what she implied about you…"

"Let it go, Lance. Don't let it get to you. We know how ridiculous her accusation is, and that's all that matters. Stay here with me and Cado and concentrate on your new business venture and being a proper father to your own son. Let Arthur and Guinevere deal with Cindy in their way. Rise above it all and show her what true dignity and strength is."

"She'll be expecting a reaction," Lance said.

"How much will she lie awake at night anticipating that reaction?" Gwyn asked. "Don't give her that satisfaction. You'll win this battle only if you don't react. Cindy obviously likes to play psychological warfare. We have King Arthur and Guinevere on our side, and she can't possibly win against them. Let Cindy say whatever she wants. All her words will return to haunt her in time. Replace her venomous words with happier thoughts. Let her be the one who's eaten up by her own malice and venom. She can't touch us as long as we remain here."

"What about my father?"

"There's nothing you can do about your father at the moment. You can offer him the hand of friendship when he needs it though. Cindy obviously believes she can get to you by turning your father against you. You should only concentrate on the things you can do something about and keep your mind off the things you have no control over."

Gwyn could always make things seem so simple. She had always preferred to sit quietly and carefully think things through. It helped her to make sense of even the most difficult of situations. Right now they needed to do nothing but continue to believe in each other. Arthur and Guinevere were the ones best positioned to deal with Cindy. They wouldn't tolerate her allegation. Gwyn believed they would let her continue for now and give her the opportunity to make an even bigger fool of herself before they were finished.

"I'd like to be there when it happens," Lance remarked. "My father wanted to force me to return to Boston. He told me I'd have to return sooner or later. He and Cindy didn't like it when I told them I've got permission to live and work here. They don't have a hold over me. I'm free from them."

Gwyn wanted him to stay here with her and Cado, where she knew he would come to no harm. He needed to show Cindy that he could, and would, succeed without his father's help. Gwyn hesitated as she stared at the ground in front of her feet.

"If you're looking for a father-figure, you could always look to your step-father. I know he unnerves you, and I have noticed how he watches you all the time. I think he's just trying too hard in his desperation to be accepted by you. Can't you try giving him a chance?"

"I don't know, Gwyn. It'd feel as though I'd be insulting my real father somehow."

"How much has your real father tried to make sure your step-father doesn't take his place? We know no one can replace him completely. What kind of father-figure has your real father been? When he did reach out to you like he should have always done, he then betrayed you again. He can't justifiably blame you if you accept a substitute who's prepared to stand by you when he's abandoned you. You're not to blame for what happened. You're not responsible for the choice your father's made. Your loyalty lies here now, with Cado and me."

Gwyn hesitated. Lance gazed at her when she continued.

"David saw King Arthur protecting you just now. Everyone did, except your father and Cindy. I don't believe your step-father is a bad person. I believe he's just trying too hard in his desperation to be accepted by you. He needs you to lighten up a little and accept he's a part of your life now. Your life will be much easier if you'll let David play his part. You have so much to gain if you'll begin to accept him. Would it really hurt you to give him a chance? I understand how hard it is for you to trust him, especially with the way he's behaving. There is a way for you to see how trustworthy he is. You only need to bring him here and introduce him to Arthur and Guinevere."

He said nothing as he thought about her suggestion. He couldn't deny that Arthur and Guinevere would know how honourable David was. They could read people's minds and know what they really thought. If he brought David here, he would then know if he could truly trust him. It had to be better than the position he was currently in.

Gwyn smiled as she stood up and encouraged him to join her. It was time for him to discover whether David had an ulterior motive to genuine friendship. Lance hesitated then stood up and looked about him one last time before they headed back to the house.

Chapter Sixteen

Gwyn and Lance hesitated before they stepped out from the trees and into the heavily falling snow. Rick, Will and Anna were standing by their cars as large snowflakes swirled around them in the blustery wind. Cado was rousing from his sleep in the adverse weather. Lance reluctantly handed him to Gwyn before he spoke briefly to the trio. He understood their eagerness to drive home before they became stranded here.

Gwyn adjusted the blanket slightly to keep Cado protected from the weather and headed for the house. He was fully awake as she climbed the stairs and shut herself in the bedroom. She sat on the chair by the window and began to feed him. He soon settled and fed quietly as she gazed out of the window. The falling snow blotted out much of the landscape and prevented her from seeing much. She hoped Blake and Cindy had successfully flown out before the blizzard had rolled in. The last thing they wanted or needed was for them to be trapped here indefinitely.

She bathed and dressed Cado when he finished feeding then made her way back downstairs. Nancy was in the living room, and Gwyn was surprised to find her alone. She settled Cado in his pram while Nancy made some coffee. She watched her son until Nancy returned and offered her a mug of coffee.

"I wonder whether David and I should leave you in peace too," Nancy said.

"You don't need to do that. It'll be Christmas in a few days. Won't you at least stay for that?"

Gwyn sat on the settee as Nancy looked away. The room was warm, with the red furniture, carpet and curtains blending well with the cream coloured walls. The tree twinkled and sparkled constantly as the lights reflected off the tinsel and baubles and the scent of pine filled the room.

"I'm not sure we should. Lance hasn't taken to David at all. I hoped he would, but he doesn't seem to want to accept him."

"Where are they?" Gwyn asked.

"They've gone over to the wood."

Gwyn smiled.

"I think they're going to be just fine. I think David has simply been trying a little too hard to be accepted. Lance has just found it all a little too much. He'll accept him when Arthur and Guinevere accept him."

Nancy gazed blankly at her, as though she was expecting a proper explanation.

"Lance is upset about having been disowned by his father after relations between them had begun to improve. Cindy has obviously come between them. I told Lance that I believe she's doing it in order to get a reaction from him. I've told him I want him to stay here with me and Cado, where I know he's safe. I've hopefully convinced him to concentrate on making his company work so everyone can see how successful he can be without his father's help. I think his being disowned by his father could be the break he needs to prove what he really is capable of achieving."

"I hope you're right."

Nancy wished Lance would talk to her in the same way he talked to Gwyn. She knew she was probably the one to blame for that though. Lance had always kept his thoughts and emotions to himself. He had built a brick wall in his mind to stop anyone getting in. Gwyn, however, was different. She was sympathetic, and she understood why he thought in the way he did. She was all too easy to talk to and be with, and that made it easy for Lance to accept and trust her judgement.

They heard the front door open when Lance and David eventually returned. They hung their coats in the hall then joined Gwyn and Nancy in the living room. The tension between them had begun to subside as Lance started to relax and accept this new person into his life. They had been to Avalon, where they had met King Arthur and Guinevere.

"Leodegrance was there too," Lance informed, "and he told me Sir Pelleas is preparing to join them."

"Leodegrance and Sir Pelleas?"

Gwyn's eyes widened. It made her wonder…

"What on earth are you talking about?" Nancy questioned.

Gwyn snapped out of her trance and explained. Leodegrance was the keeper of the Round Table, and he was also Guinevere's father. Sir Pelleas was one of the Knights of the Round Table. His wife, the Lady Vivien, was the Lady of the lake.

"Maybe now that Morgan is safely locked away she'll be released from the spell trapping her in the water. Perhaps she'll be able to return to her original form and join her husband again."

"Maybe they'll help sort Cindy out," Lance blurted out, "with her saying we're guaranteed to fail because I'm involved. She's just showing her ignorance. She has no idea who she's dealing with. She has no idea what Arthur and Guinevere are going to do to her as punishment for her suggestions against us."

Nancy's mind was spinning.

"What's going on? What on earth have Arthur and Guinevere got to do with this?"

Lance had forgotten about his mother and step-father's presence. He hesitated then decided to explain so he had some control over exactly how much was revealed.

"Cindy made an allegation about Gwyn and me, which effectively means she's also made the same allegation against Arthur and Guinevere. They're not going to tolerate that. Gwyn was right that I shouldn't give Cindy the reaction she wants. I'll let Arthur and Guinevere deal with her. I'll stay here with Gwyn and Cado and concentrate on what we're capable of achieving with our company. Cindy can gloat as much as she wants, she's not going to get the reaction she wants. She'll undoubtedly be incited by that more than anything. She'll become obsessed with getting a reaction from me."

Nancy stared at him. He had never behaved like this before. He was focused and determined to achieve all he was setting out to do. Gwyn watched in silence. She was glad the attention was diverted away from her. Lance, with his new-found resolve, was the one who Nancy and David were looking at. He was bold, and he had even stood up to Blake and Cindy.

Lance wasn't the one who had challenged Blake and Cindy. That person was King Arthur. The mighty king had, through Lance, made his stance so he could protect them all. He was as incensed as Lance when Gwyn and Cado had been threatened by Blake, and he was as equally incensed when Cindy had cast aspersions on them all.

"I'm glad you're standing up for yourself," Nancy said. "I doubt Blake will remain silent though."

"He told me I had to return to Boston when my visa expires, but I told him that I'm allowed to stay and work here for as long as I want. He didn't say much, and Cindy looked as though she hated the thought. It's almost as though she'd planned to make me pay for what happened before when she thought I'd have to return."

"Maybe you are much safer here," Nancy sighed. "Perhaps it'd be best if you don't return to Boston, especially while Blake's with Cindy. I can't believe he's actually going to marry her."

"He's going to leave everything to her, whether they marry or not," Lance reminded, "and that's exactly what we expected to happen. We have enough to think about with our own company for me to worry about my father though. I'll just do the same as he did. I'll help to build our company up from nothing."

"Lance, Blake wasn't the one who built his company up from nothing. He paid other people peanuts to do that for him. It wasn't his blood, sweat and toil that created what he has today. And what's more, he callously tossed those people aside when he'd finished using them."

"It wasn't that bad, Nancy."

David noticed how Lance stared at him in shocked disbelief. He looked embarrassed and uncomfortable as he realised what he had just blurted out.

"It's true," Nancy insisted. "Everything that Blake's empire is built upon is David's ideas, sweat and toil. David's the one with the knowledge and understanding. Blake's the one who managed to scrape together enough money to pay him. And with Blake being Blake, he insisted to it all being done in his name. As soon as the firm was established, he told David he had no further use for him."

David couldn't look directly at Lance as he smiled nervously.

"It wasn't so bad. Others had seen what I'd done. It was easy enough for me to find alternative work. It was no big deal, and I'm not the least bit bitter. I learned to let it go and enjoy the life I did have. It sounds as though you're preparing to do the same thing, Lance. You're nothing like Blake at all. You all deserve to succeed with all the hard work you've already put in. There is one thing that concerns me though. I fear Blake and Cindy crushing you before you get the chance to succeed."

Lance shook his head and smiled quietly. They had the support of King Arthur and Guinevere. With their help, they couldn't fail. David gazed at him and resisted the urge to argue as he remembered his earlier experience. There had been something about those apparitions he had met. There had been a sense of power and a sense of being able to achieve anything they wanted to achieve. He had, at the same time, sensed that Guinevere could delve deep into his mind and see his darkest secret. She unnerved him, and yet at the same time she soothed those nerves. He didn't doubt that Lance was protected here. He was shielded from anything to be thrown at him. He could support his wife and son in safety here.

Gwyn was quiet and confident as she sat beside her husband. Lance really did have no other choice but to stay right here.

Chapter Seventeen

Gwyn settled Cado in his crib then climbed into bed and nestled in Lance's arms. She felt safe, warm and comfortable as she rested her head on his shoulder. Her mind, however, was full of thoughts that stopped her from sleeping. She eventually broke the silence.

"You seem to be getting on better with your step-father now," she said.

"He's not so bad. My taking him to meet Arthur and Guinevere was the right thing to do. It helped me see things more clearly. He's not trying to replace my father. He could never do that. He's nothing like my father, and I don't want him to be either. I can't believe how my father treated him. I didn't know my father had treated anyone like that."

"Maybe it'd be best if you don't think about it. Your step-father's certainly not doing that. He's moved on and he's carved out a different life for himself. Please don't let any bitterness dominate your life. You can't change what's already happened, but you can influence the future."

Lance smiled as he sensed her gazing at him.

"You know, David knows an awful lot about computers. It's OK, I'm not planning on using him just so I can seek revenge on my father and Cindy. As you've already pointed out, I don't need to do anything. Arthur and Guinevere will do whatever's necessary to punish Cindy for everything she says and does. It'll then be my father's choice to decide whether to accept my offer of friendship or not. I can't force him to accept me again, and I'll be able to live with the consequences if he chooses not to. I'll survive and do well regardless of whether he's by my side or not. I have more than I need right here. I have you and Cado, and I'll have Avalon too soon."

"I'm not entirely sure it is Avalon that's going to come here," Gwyn admitted. "I can't be certain. I'll need to go and see Arthur and Guinevere before I can be sure. But what you said earlier, about Leodegrance and Sir Pelleas… I can't help but wonder if it's Camelot that's set to come here…"

She sensed him staring at her through the darkness as he sat up and twisted round slightly to face her properly.

"Camelot?"

"I can't be certain. But Leodegrance is, after all, the keeper of the Round Table. What you said earlier has suggested the return of Camelot instead of Avalon—unless they both return. It'll all depend upon how much Cindy offends Arthur and Guinevere. If she really offends them then they'll want to summon some of the knights. They'll need to be at Camelot to do that. I'll only know if I ask Arthur and Guinevere. There's no immediate hurry though. Nothing's likely to happen for a while yet, if it happens at all. It's just a possibility and nothing more. There's nothing definite about a return of Camelot. It'll only do that if Arthur calls it. It might just be that King Leodegrance has joined them so they're ready and prepared if Arthur does need to call upon it."

"Do you really think he'll summon the knights just because of what Cindy's saying?"

"Not if it's just that one comment she's already made. Arthur and Guinevere are perfectly capable of punishing her for that. It all depends upon what else she says, and it's pretty certain that she will. The more she does say then the greater the chance of Arthur summoning the knights. It's only a thought though, and it's probably just my imagination running wild. I expect it'll just be Avalon returning. Maybe it'd be best to forget I ever said anything."

"I can't do that, not now you've made the suggestion. Wouldn't that be something worth experiencing; fancy being able to actually walk around Camelot and be in the court of Arthur and Guinevere. You know it's weird, but I'm sure Guinevere looked at David in the same way she looked at Rick the other day. It's as though she knows he's hiding something. She's not said anything though, so I guess it can't be anything important."

Gwyn smiled and nestled against him when he lay back down again. She knew he was thinking about what she had just told him. He would undoubtedly think about it a lot over the next few days. It was a natural thing to do. She wasn't convinced herself that Camelot wouldn't return. She absent-mindedly stroked Lance's skin as she too thought about the possibility until they eventually fell asleep.

A thick layer of snow had covered the ground by the time the sun rose the following morning. Gwyn gazed out at the scene as she fed Cado. She handed him to Lance when he was finished and had changed his nappy. She then showered. Lance was staring outside and barely glanced round when she joined him again. The snow's surface glistened beneath the watery sunshine. She smiled quietly as she gazed out at it.

"I don't expect the others will join us today," she said. "It'll be too dangerous for them to drive over until the roads are cleared. Maybe it'd be best if they don't come back until after Christmas."

Lance looked horrified as panic took a hold.

"I can't manage without them. I can't do everything on my own."

"Lance, you're more than capable of dealing with any orders or requests, assuming that is that you'll be able to get out to post them off."

Lance stared at her as he slowly realised what she was suggesting. If the others couldn't get here then he wouldn't be able to get out. They didn't need this, not when they were just starting out. His mind raced as he began to think out loud as he logically solved the problem. He could only acknowledge and promise to fulfil any orders when they got the chance. Gwyn smiled and reached across so she could kiss him. She knew he was more than capable of dealing with things. He only needed to quell his initial panic and think things through before he took any action. He only needed to phone Rick or Will if he did need help. He could deal with this by himself. He could show Blake and Cindy he was more than capable of running a successful business. They would not, and could not, defeat him.

Lance settled Cado in his pram then joined Gwyn in the kitchen. She was cooking their breakfast. He made some coffee before they sat at the table and ate. He then headed to the office and left her to clear the table. She cleaned her teeth and made the bed. She was loading the washing machine when Nancy and David joined her. Nancy sounded surprised that the others hadn't arrived yet.

"We're not expecting them today," Gwyn told her. "I don't suppose they'll be here until the roads have been cleared."

"But you've had barely a couple of inches of snow!" Nancy exclaimed. "This is nothing compared to what we get at home. How can everything come to a standstill by a couple of inches?"

"It's just the way things are here," Gwyn smiled. "We're not exactly in a built-up area here. Clearing the road here won't be a high priority. It'll be different in Bristol, if they've had any snow. Those roads will be cleared."

"I suppose."

Nancy reluctantly conceded defeat as she began to cook breakfast for herself and David. Gwyn moved on to housework then headed to the living room and checked Cado. He was sleeping peacefully, giving her the chance to pick up her embroidery and thread her needle. She had barely started stitching when a movement in the doorway attracted her attention. Lance had done everything he could. He had nothing left to do but join her. He couldn't work on, not with the others not being here.

Will was the person who developed new programmes, so he felt as though he couldn't even do that. The business enquiries had increased at an alarmingly fast rate as word had spread. They were already beginning to build up a good reputation. Lance suddenly wondered what they would be doing now if they developed for the domestic market too. He stared into space as he thought about the possibility. Maybe he should suggest it when the others eventually returned.

Why shouldn't they branch out into the domestic market as well? There was no law preventing it, and he was sure there had to be thousands of people looking for cheap and simple software.

He continued to stare into space as he sat beside Gwyn. They had ignored a massive market—a market that Blake and Cindy believed was insignificant and worthless. The more he thought about it, the more he wanted to discuss it with Rick and Will. Maybe he should even have a go at developing a simple programme himself. It had to be better than sitting here and doing nothing.

"Where're mom and David?" he suddenly asked.

"They wanted to see what the hills look like in the snow."

"Oh. Do you think David will give me a hand to develop some new software?"

"I can ask him when he gets back and send him through if he agrees," Gwyn said.

Lance nodded. He just lacked confidence, and they both knew that. Gwyn knew he was more than capable of designing software. He just needed the opportunity to prove it. She watched him disappear then settled to her stitching again. She had a feeling David would be more than willing to work alongside Lance. This was the perfect opportunity for them to build up the friendship David was seeking. This snowfall could help them far more than any of them realised.

She knew Arthur and Guinevere had already begun to help them build up their business. She now had a feeling that, by the time the others returned, Lance's confidence would have grown immensely with David's help and encouragement. She smiled as she continued her stitching in silence. She believed Lance was about to discover a hidden talent that would prove to be both popular and successful. Blake and Cindy would be lost for words, and it would serve them right. This snowfall was exactly what Lance needed.

Chapter Eighteen

Nancy and David dropped off their cases and collected their boarding passes before they turned away from the desk and walked across to Lance. He had reluctantly stayed here after Nancy had stopped him from returning home when she dropped them off. She wanted to talk to him, and Lance was dreading the impending conversation.

Nancy led the way through the airport terminal to a coffee shop and sat down at an empty table. She let Lance buy their coffees. He noticed how tense and a little nervous David looked as he put the tray on the table. His mother was behaving normally. She picked up a mug of coffee and sipped it before she put it back down again.

"I'm worried about you, Lance," she said. "I'm not denying Gwyn's a lovely girl, but this obsession with King Arthur... I mean, it's not normal, and she's pulling you into it all too. And as for this ridiculous name you've given my grandson..."

"It's not an obsession, mom, and Cado's name isn't ridiculous."

"I'm serious, Lance. You've changed, and it's scaring me."

"How can you say that after what you saw happen? How can you call it ridiculous or an obsession?"

"I remember what happened, but you obviously don't know how much it freaked me out. I can't explain what happened, and it shouldn't be accepted without question. With the way you're now behaving, it's little wonder you're being called eccentric..."

"Mom, why can't you see what's happening? You more than most people should understand. You were there at the time, and you saw what happened. It was my choice. I chose to accept him and the responsibility that comes with it. My life's going in that direction now. I can't change my mind, even if I did want to."

"But, Lance, can't you see how it looks to me? I mean, this suggestion that someone from hundreds of years ago has come back in you. And as for that embroidery Gwyn's stitching… her claim that her mom designed it is really creepy. Why doesn't she just admit she did it?"

"Because she didn't, mom. I was there when she found those designs, and so were Laura and Melissa."

"Oh come on, Lance! She could've easily hidden it when you were out."

"Laura pointed out that they're in Gwyn's mom's handwriting. You can say what you want, but you can't change the fact her mom drew those four designs. The only explanation is Gwyn's explanation."

"That her mom's hand was guided by Guinevere? How could she possibly know you existed, let alone turn up there?"

"I don't know. You could also ask how they could've possibly known about the house. There're a lot of things that have happened that can't be explained. I've chosen to accept it all, and I believe I'm better off because of it. I believe I was supposed to accept Arthur. You can say what you like, but I'm glad I'm not working for my father any longer. I'm glad we're doing our own thing, and I don't care if people think I'm eccentric. I'm going to do things my way."

"Well, I'm not happy about the influence Gwyn has over you. And what about that poor child. What about my grandson? He has to live with that ridiculous name you've given him."

Lance stared at her.

"You wouldn't think it's ridiculous if you knew its meaning. I don't know how you can criticise after you never bothered with me as I was growing up. I'm sorry, mom, I've no regrets for what I've done. I'm going home before you can insult me further. Have a safe journey."

He stood up and walked away. David caught up with him just before he stepped outside.

"I'm sorry about your mom," he said. "I'll talk to her and see if I can't get her to see things from your side. If it's any consolation, I don't think you're eccentric at all."

"Thanks, and I'm sorry. I didn't mean to cause any friction between you and mom."

"I can handle your mom easily enough. What is the significance of Cado's name?"

Lance eyed him for a few moments.

"It's the name of the knight who helped Arthur rescue Guinevere after she'd been kidnapped."

"It sounds like a very honourable name."

Lance smiled politely. He didn't know whether he was being serious or patronising.

"Thank you for all your help and support. I appreciate it."

"It was a pleasure. I enjoyed working with you, and I hope we'll be able to do it again sometime."

"I'd like that."

He suddenly looked embarrassed. He quickly turned and hurried away, leaving David to face Nancy alone.

Gwyn pushed the pram along the lane on her way to the general store in the nearby village. A wintery dampness filled the air, and a chill wind blew straight through the leafless trees and hedgerows. The others were moving their equipment from the house to the newly-finished office in the outbuilding. The conversion was complete, and the group were pleased with the work done.

The software programmes that Lance had developed with David's encouragement were already beginning to sell. Lance had something to focus upon, and he now had a sense of actually giving some input to the company. He wasn't like his father, who had given nothing at all. He didn't feel worthless after all. He had become a more valuable member to the team.

Gwyn posted off the packages she had when she reached the store. She then bought the provisions she wanted, stepped back out into the cold, damp air and headed towards home. She knew Cado would soon waken for a feed, and she wanted to get back home before he did. The occasional car passed her as she walked, while the last of the snow stubbornly lingered in the shadows. It was late in February, and warmer air was still a few weeks away. Everything for now was just damp and dismal, and the atmosphere was wet without it actually raining.

Cado woke as she walked along the lane. It spurred her on as she guessed he felt cold. His initial moans and whimpers became a loud crying and screaming by the time she reached home. She pushed the pram indoors and put a bottle of milk in a pan of water to warm. She then took off her coat and boots and picked Cado up. He was rigid with frustration, distress and hunger. He slowly relaxed as he began to gulp down the milk.

She sat on a kitchen chair while she fed him, and she looked up when the door opened and Lance stepped inside. He looked concerned, but he relaxed when told Cado was just hungry. He hesitated then began to make some coffee.

"Your receipt is in the bag," Gwyn said. "I expect Anna will want it. How's the move going?"

"It's going really slowly. Will's setting up the computers again at the moment. I can't believe how much stuff we have. I'm sure we didn't have this much when we started, and that's only three months ago."

Gwyn smiled as she looked down at Cado again. He looked more like Lance now. Anyone could see that. She gazed at him then looked back up and caught Lance watching her.

"What's wrong?" she asked.

"Nothing's wrong at all. You're so different to Cindy. You'd never leave Cado with a nanny while you fly off to another country."

She smiled softly. She should be offended by his comment, but she knew what he meant. They didn't need to go anywhere. They had everything they needed and wanted right here. They only needed to go into the wood. Lance suddenly looked embarrassed as he put a mug of coffee on the table in front of her. He didn't want to leave her. He wanted to stay right here with her. He knew he had to return to the others instead though.

He hesitated then turned and picked up the tray. Gwyn would undoubtedly be busy caring for Cado and preparing dinner, and he really should be at work with the others. Gwyn watched him go. She finished feeding Cado, drank her coffee then settled her son in his pram in the living room. She put dinner on to cook then returned to the living room and gazed out of the window.

The garden was wet and overgrown. The grass and weeds were one big, tangled mess within the confines of their natural stone wall. She was looking beyond it all though. She was looking at the hills on the other side of the garden wall. She would give anything to be out on those hills. She was a virtual prisoner in her own home. Cado was too young and too vulnerable to the adverse weather. She couldn't take him out for too long. She could only stare out at the heavy mist that covered the hillside. She smiled again. She belonged here, and she knew it. She'd have never felt completely comfortable or happy in Boston. She was glad and thankful that Lance had realised he too belonged here. She was glad that he had decided to stay here.

She didn't take much notice of the others moving between the house and office after dinner. She was too pre-occupied with Cado and her embroidery to watch them. The afternoon eventually passed, and the trio drove away and left Lance to join Gwyn in the house. He felt as though the day had dragged. It was finally over at last. The atmosphere was relaxed as they sat in the living room.

"We need to go into the wood tomorrow," Gwyn suddenly said. "Arthur and Guinevere want us to be there when Avalon returns. No one's going to stop the others if they want to join us. We need to be a part of the return though."

Lance held her a little more tightly and kissed the side of her head.

"I wouldn't miss it for anything," he told her. "Nothing's going to keep me away. As long as we're there, I don't care what the others do."

It was going to be a momentous occasion, of that he was certain. They had to be there, of that there was no question.

Chapter Nineteen

Gwyn felt a little self-conscious as she opened the door and stepped into the office. She held Cado in her arms and watched as Lance joined her while the others watched them.

"We'll stay here," Rick said. "We don't want to intrude. We think it's best just you two go. We're not comfortable about accepting your invitation."

Gwyn gazed at him for a few moments then nodded. Maybe it would be best if only they went on this occasion. She and Lance let themselves out of the office and headed to the nearby trees. The other three watched from one of the windows until they disappeared into the wood.

"Come and watch what happens," Rick urged.

"I don't know that…"

"Come on, Anna. It'll help you to understand their behaviour a lot better. It'll do you both good to see what we've got working on our side."

Gwyn and Lance stopped in a very specific spot. Trees grew all around them. Neither of them knew what to expect. They just knew they had to be here at this very spot so they could play their part in what was about to happen. They were needed here, of that they were certain. Nothing would happen without them being present.

The pair glanced at each other then looked ahead of them again. They could sense the other three stopping in the trees behind them. They had decided to come after all. Their presence, however, was unimportant. They posed no threat, and their presence made no difference to what was about to happen.

Nothing did happen for a few moments. The trees then began to slowly melt away before their very eyes. More light shone down as a large clearing opened up before them. A brilliant white light then suddenly pierced skywards without warning from the cleared ground. An eerie mist entered the clearing, which moved and swirled constantly before eventually drifting away from the edges of the newly-formed clearing. It revealed a lake as it drew back where trees had grown moments before.

The dazzling white light gradually faded to a comfortable level. It continued to shine, just like it had done once before. It was all here again—the island in the centre of the lake in a wood. Avalon had returned. Gwyn and Lance gazed at the mist-shrouded island and said nothing. A simple and familiar boat was gliding effortlessly towards them through the water. A hand was, at the same time, slowly and gracefully rising up out of the water. Droplets of water shimmered in the peaceful white light as they fell back into the lake. The boat drew level, and Arthur took what the hand offered. The boat then continued on, while the hand slipped gracefully back into the water's depths, and stopped beside Gwyn and Lance at the shore of the lake.

King Arthur stepped out of the boat and offered a steadying hand to his queen as Guinevere joined him. They stood on the pale green grass and waited patiently as Gwyn and Lance stepped forwards. They had returned, and it marked the end of their exile. The mighty king and his queen knew Gwyn and Lance had had no choice but to return the necklace and chain to the waters of the lake. It was the only way of protecting them all. The danger had passed, and there was nothing to threaten them now. It was safe for them to return and be reunited once again.

Gwyn and Lance gazed at Arthur and Guinevere and focused on the chain and necklace they were holding. Arthur had retrieved them from the Lady Vivien when they sailed across the water. The mighty king and his queen were now offering them to the people before them. The exchange was different this time. It was just a simple handing over from one to the other. This time the light shone constantly. There was no increase in intensity, and no being blinded as this transfer took place. The light simply continued to shine steadily and evenly upon the lake and surrounding trees.

The deed accomplished, Guinevere smiled and gently stroked Cado's head before stepping back onto the boat. Arthur remained on the bank as he gazed down at Gwyn.

"You're right," he told her. "My father-in-law has joined us just in case I need to call upon the services of the knights. Only then will Camelot return. It'll be the last resort. It'll only be summoned if all else has failed."

"And Sir Pelleas?" Lance asked.

Guinevere gazed at him from the boat.

"He and the Lady Vivien have suffered enough. It's time for the Lady Vivien to return to her original form, thanks to your beliefs and actions taming Morgan. It's time for her and Sir Pelleas to be reunited once again. They've served us well, and this is their reward for their loyalty. There's nothing to fear. The Lady Vivien has taught the water nymphs well. Avalon will still be well protected."

Arthur took over, drawing Lance's attention away from Guinevere.

"You have more than enough to concentrate on. Cindy has already noticed your success. She's going to return soon and attempt to destroy your new-found confidence with her words of spite and venom. We will always be with you now, no matter where you might be. Don't ever doubt your ability. Just remember not to mention your new-found ally just yet. She believes you've had a lot of help from someone. She can't accept you've achieved this with just a little encouragement. You'll know when the time is right to reveal the identity of your ally."

King Arthur smiled kindly at Lance as he stepped back onto the boat alongside his queen. The boat drifted away, after having remained steady and still against the bank, and glided sedately across the lake towards the island. Gwyn and Lance watched as it disappeared into the mist. They then looked at each other, and she rested against him when he slid an arm around her waist. They were united once more, just like they had been before. It was time to return home.

They turned and gazed at the three people standing in the trees. Anna looked pale and stunned, as though she found it impossible to take in what she had just seen. Surely this wasn't possible. How could this lake suddenly appear like this where trees had once stood? Gwyn smiled and gently coaxed her away. She sat her in the kitchen and, having warmed a bottle of milk, began to feed Cado as she explained.

The island in the lake was Avalon. It had returned to them again. It was hidden in a wood on the hills once, but last year was in danger. The only way for them to protect it had been for them to throw their necklace and chain into the water. They were gifts from Arthur and Guinevere, and the link enabled them to live on through Gwyn and Lance. They were the link to the modern world, and Arthur and Guinevere's chance to return from the Otherworld. They had brought Gwyn and Lance together, and they protected them despite Avalon remaining their home.

"But what happened just now doesn't make any sense," Anna objected.

"Sometimes it's best not to try to make any logical sense out of things. They simply can't be explained. They just happen, and they're best accepted as they are. It's going to happen a lot around here now. Arthur and Guinevere need us to survive, so they too survive. They'll ensure we do that and prosper. They're not pleased with Cindy's remarks. Those comments have been made against Arthur and Guinevere as well as Lance and me. They'll only tolerate it for so long before she's silenced. She'll then be punished for every remark she'll make. We've been told she's going to return soon and try to defame Lance. We'll need to keep quiet and not retaliate. Arthur and Guinevere have everything under control. They'll make sure she doesn't go unpunished."

Anna wasn't convinced. How could two ghosts from days of old punish someone existing on this earth? She didn't know if she could not react to someone as abhorrent as Cindy Peterson. Lance, however, did have more reason than anyone to loathe her. Anna guessed that, if he could bite his tongue, she would also have to do so. Gwyn smiled. Arthur would be here with Lance at all times to protect him.

"Try to remember that by saying nothing, Cindy will be enraged. She won't be getting the reaction she's seeking, and that'll really infuriate her. She'll end up being the one who's indignant and offended. She'll be reacting in the way she wants Lance to. The more she mocks Lance, then the bigger the fool she'll look when her downfall inevitably comes. Say nothing and let Arthur and Guinevere deal with her. They know what they're doing. And don't say anything about David's help. Cindy knows nothing about that. We need her to believe it's all the work of just Lance, Rick and Will. Lance will reveal David's support when the time is right."

Anna gazed at her. Every indication of their success pointed to Gwyn's claims being true. She knew no one would believe her if she said anything, and she could understand why. She had just witnessed the return of Avalon though. She had seen the two people crossing over to them. She had seen the necklace and chain given to Gwyn and Lance.

Anna stared at the delicate and intricate Celtic cross necklace that hung around Gwyn's neck. No one could make any sense out of what had just happened. Happen it had though. There was no denying that, and she couldn't ignore what she had seen. There was no logical explanation. She just had the explanation given by Gwyn. Could it really be true? Gwyn's explanation, as fantastical as it seemed, did somehow make sense. Could King Arthur, Guinevere and Avalon really exist? She had always assumed it was a myth that some people, including Gwyn, profited from. She now knew how real the myth was. It was very real indeed.

Chapter Twenty

Nancy and David stayed in Boston over Easter so she could revel in the success of her shop. Blake and Cindy, however, were spotted in Bristol. Gwyn was venturing outside with Cado more now the air felt warmer and he was growing stronger in the lengthening days. The small garden in front of the house was cleared, and the grass seed that had been sown now gave a green hue to the soil. They had all the time in the world to watch the grass grow, as time here seemed to stand still.

Lance locked the office at the end of the day before Good Friday. He joined Gwyn and Cado in the house as Will and Anna drove away. They pushed all thoughts of work to the very back of their minds for the long weekend. They had four days before being due back at work again, and Lance was going to spend them with Gwyn and Cado.

Gwyn had worked with the landscape gardeners as they had toiled tirelessly for days. The tangled mess of grass and bramble was now cleared away to reveal a large expanse of back garden. They had come across nothing worth salvaging, so they had stripped everything from within the boundary of the wall. The soil had been dug and raked level before a patio was laid and grass seed raked into the tilled earth.

Gwyn and Lance stood on the patio after eating their dinner. A vast expanse of the garden looked barren and brown. They both knew the grass seed would soon start to grow and change the colour to green. Two cherry tree saplings and three rosemary bushes were at the far end of the garden. They looked small and insignificant against the wall and hills. In time though the trees would grow tall and dwarf the bushes.

Gwyn smiled as a warm glow spread through her. Floral borders stretched along the two side walls, and both were filled with a mixture of forget-me-nots, lavender, thyme, sweet cicely and sweet rocket. She knew the garden would be transformed every time the sun set and the moon shone down. In time, the borders would fill with a large array of flowers. In time, the garden would only improve. It all only needed time. In another year, they would be able to enjoy this garden.

Cado was awake for much longer periods of time now. He was crawling too, and the toddler sought more attention from his father. Lance revelled in the time he had with his young son. He was determined to share in a normal childhood as he played with Cado. He was going to spend the next four days experiencing a childhood he had never known.

The long weekend flew by. All too soon Tuesday dawned. The day felt relatively warm with a blue sky. Will and Anna arrived and joined Lance in the office. Rick and Melissa were in Greece with their daughters for the school holiday, leaving the trio to check for orders and start work. Everything continued as normal, despite Rick's absence. Anna had a large stack of packets to post by the time Gwyn put her head around the door.

"I'm just going to the village," she announced. "Is there anything you want?"

"We could do with some coffee," Anna said. "I'll come with you so I can post this lot."

She quickly gathered up the packets and headed to the nearby village with Gwyn. Cado was awake and alert and taking everything in as he looked about him. He missed nothing, even when in the store. Gwyn did her shopping while Anna dealt with the post. They then took their time as they walked back along the country lane. They soaked up the warmth in the air and smelt the many scents carried on the breeze. Spring had arrived. The trees and hedgerows were in bud and bursting with life while flowers brought splashes of colour around them. The air was clean and fresh and the pace of life slower compared to the city.

"It's lovely here isn't it," Anna said. "It's so calm and peaceful. I wonder whether Will would like to live here."

Gwyn smiled. Anna was a country girl at heart, yet she also liked living in the city with its shops and nightlife. Gwyn wasn't sure about Will. He had lived in Bristol for all of his life. She couldn't imagine him adjusting to life outside the city. Anna gazed at every house they passed and wondered what it would be like to live there. They were all very different to their mid-terraced house in Bristol.

"Maybe you should look into it," Gwyn suggested. "Weigh up the pros and cons and work out the costs before you suggest anything to Will."

They stepped off the country lane with its traffic and followed the track to the house. They could see the hills in the distance, and they could even make out the people walking across them. Easter marked the beginning of the summer season, and there certainly appeared to be plenty of people about. There was more traffic on the road now, which meant more cars dodging around them when they made the short journey to the village store.

Gwyn and Anna suddenly fell silent for a few moments when they spotted and recognised the extra car parked in the yard. It was Blake's company car, and Graham undoubtedly felt both embarrassed and uncomfortable. He was in a difficult and almost intolerable position. Gwyn and Anna looked at each other then continued on their way.

Lance and Will were standing just outside the office door. They were making a united stance against the immaculately turned out blonde woman standing before them. Cindy Peterson was here. Gwyn and Anna caught her eye as they drew nearer. She looked them up and down then smirked with disdain as she chose to ignore them.

"Take no notice of her," Gwyn spoke quietly. "Just go straight into the office and let the men deal with her."

Gwyn walked on as Anna followed her advice. She pushed the pram into the garden then turned to close the gate behind her. She hadn't expected to be followed, but Cindy was right behind her. Their unwelcome visitor had been talking to Lance and Will when Gwyn had walked past her.

The conversation had come to an abrupt end, and Gwyn was now face to face with her.

She sensed Guinevere's reassuring presence, and that moral support gave her confidence. She wasn't feeling the least bit intimidated by Cindy standing before her. High heels gave Cindy the advantage of a few extra inches. Her designer clothes were pressed to perfection. Her hair, as always, was professionally styled. Her hands were manicured and the air was filled with the strong scent of liberally-applied expensive perfume. There was no doubt that Cindy spent a lot of time making sure she was always immaculately turned out. She took a lot of pride in her appearance. Every last and miniscule detail revealed everything had to be perfect, and money was no object when striving for that goal.

Gwyn's eyes were soft and patient as she gazed at Cindy. She was comfortable with who she was. She certainly didn't obsess about her appearance. Gwyn knew that, when compared to Cindy, almost everyone looked dowdy and plain. Gwyn was the one who Lance had chosen to marry and spend the rest of his life with though. She had won that battle, despite making no real effort with her appearance. Other things were far more important than how she looked to her.

Cindy looked Gwyn up and down and took in every little detail. She displayed a complete lack of respect towards her as she did so. Gwyn, however, didn't care. She wasn't at all interested in what Cindy thought of her. Cindy spoke at last, and she ensured her remarks were loud enough for everyone to hear.

"So, you're the famous Gwyn. I don't doubt for a moment that Lance has told you all about me."

She glanced round to check whether Lance had emerged from the office again. She then appeared irritated about getting no reaction. Gwyn remained calm, her voice quiet and steady when she answered.

"If he has, then it didn't take long. We prefer to discuss things that we find far more interesting."

Cindy scowled. She hated not being the topic of conversation. She was determined to not be beaten by this lowly and plain country girl standing before her. She decided to gloat.

"Oh there're so many things I could tell you. You really should be interested in them. Do you know Lance had the audacity to cheat on me all the time?"

Gwyn didn't look the least bit interested. Cindy, in contrast, became increasingly annoyed by not getting the reaction she craved. She couldn't possibly let this simple person beat her. She was just a simple country girl who possessed no make-up, and she undoubtedly didn't know how to apply it properly. Cindy was convinced that, for that reason alone, Gwyn couldn't possibly possess the intelligence needed to succeed in the cut-throat business world. She was somehow managing to make Cindy feel as though she was the inadequate one though. There was something about this peasant that didn't ring true, and that unnerved her. Cindy was determined not to be beaten. She had, after all, already shown she would resort to anything to ensure she was always victorious.

"Has he insisted on a paternity test yet?"

Cindy was unaware of the sudden sense of hostility towards her. She had angered the ghosts of old with her question. She continued on. The hostility returned as a strange semi-darkness surrounded them.

"He doesn't trust anyone. He'll never believe he's the father. I doubt he could even father a child. He's not even capable of achieving that. He'll drag you into court and bring someone else along to prove he's not responsible."

Gwyn had watched Lance approach them and stop just behind Cindy. He heard every word spoken, and he now stepped forwards to stand beside their foe.

"It has nothing to do with you whether a paternity test has been done or not. That's something that is, and always will be, between just Gwyn and me."

Cindy smirked casually and defiantly as she stared at him. She was convinced by his statement that a test had already been carried out. She believed she had won, and she couldn't help but gloat.

"Lance and Gwyn," she remarked. "Lancelot and Guinevere. I suppose you think you're made for each other."

The air cooled significantly while the darkness intensified. King Arthur was showing his indignation. The darkness then lifted and warmth returned as Guinevere reassured him. Cindy had actually sensed the king's displeasure this time. She quickly looked about her and began to nervously move away. She then stopped a little too closely for comfort to Lance. He, however, refused to back away. Arthur's presence gave him the confidence to stand his ground. Cindy had just shown her ignorance while in noble company.

"You're not to come here again," he told her. "You're not welcome."

"There's nothing worth coming for," she commented. "Just make the most of this brief success you're currently enjoying. I'll make sure it doesn't last. I'll find out who's helping you and put a stop to it."

"You're looking for someone who doesn't exist. It's about time you accepted that maybe, I am actually capable of developing software."

He gazed steadily at her while silently daring her to disbelieve him. Cindy laughed harshly.

"What a ludicrous idea! This is me you're talking to, and I know how useless you are. You couldn't possibly do something like that without any help."

Lance managed to remain calm.

"It's surprising what people can do when given the chance isn't it. I really can't thank you enough, by the way, for turning my father against me. It's given me this opportunity to show everyone what I'm really capable of achieving. I'd have never been given this chance if I was still being controlled by my father. Life is so much nicer without him around."

Cindy's features twisted and contorted as she scowled again. She had no ready answer this time. She could only begrudgingly admit he had beaten her on this occasion.

"It's all doomed to failure," she insisted. "I'll make sure it does, even if it's the last thing I do."

She turned and strutted back to the car. Lance stayed by Gwyn's side as they watched her leave. They had the support of Arthur and Guinevere. They couldn't possibly fail with such powerful allies. Cindy was just trying to make him doubt his ability. Gwyn broke the silence.

"You're not going to fail."

"I know. She's not done herself any favours today. There's not going to be a paternity test. I don't need to prove I'm Cado's father."

"I know, just like I also know you'll never cheat on me. Don't let her get to you, Lance. Don't let her win."

Lance smiled as he looked at her. With her by his side, Cindy could never win.

Chapter Twenty-One

Lance reluctantly disappeared into the bathroom and showered while Gwyn bottle-fed Cado. Easter, and Cindy's venomous words, was a distant memory. She had brought them closer together instead of driving a wedge between them with her malicious suggestions. She had attempted to stir up trouble, but she had failed. Her claim that he was incapable of achieving anything had been proved wrong. The demand for their software had increased with each passing day, and it had kept Lance pre-occupied and focused. And then Nancy had phoned…

Today was the day on which Cindy had chosen to marry Blake. It was also Lance and Gwyn's first wedding anniversary. The ceremony, by all accounts, was to be large and extremely lavish. Lance expected nothing less from Cindy. He believed it to be a cheap and tacky stunt that was aimed at getting a reaction from him. He had been indignant at first, but then Gwyn had talked to him. They had received no invitation, and nothing to take them to Boston.

Gwyn finished feeding Cado. She changed his nappy and dressed him then let him go as Lance joined then again. Cado immediately rolled over and crawled away from her. He then pulled himself up onto his feet when he reached the first useful piece of furniture. Gwyn smiled, stood up and left him in Lance's care so she too could have a shower. Lance was still in the bedroom when she returned to brush and dry her hair. She tied her hair back out of the way and was at last ready to follow Lance downstairs.

He picked Cado up and carried him to the kitchen. He secured him into his high chair then made some coffee while Gwyn handed a rusk to Cado and cooked breakfast. Nancy and David were visiting. They too had been snubbed, and they hadn't wanted to be in Boston on the day of this wedding. Cindy had chosen to invite only the people she wanted to attend. Cado had grown so much since Christmas, and Nancy and David could see how he looked more like Lance as he grew.

Two new pictures hung on one of the walls in the living room. Nancy had noticed them as soon as she had walked into the room. One was the picture of Lance designed by Gwyn's mother. He really did look like the person in the picture with his longer, more tousled hair and informal clothing. The likeness unnerved Nancy visibly. No one could explain how Gwyn's mother could have known, and no one could argue with the result. Gwyn had merely stitched the chart left to her.

The second picture was the one of Gwyn. Her mother had put a simple silver coronet on her head. No one questioned this picture. It was just her mother teasing her from beyond the grave. She was used to being teased affectionately and gently. They had always made light of her likeness to the queen, despite knowing the gravity of her pre-destined life.

Lance was banned from the office today. The other three had refused to let him join them. He was to spend the day with Gwyn today so they could celebrate their first wedding anniversary together. The others were already in the office when Gwyn and Lance emerged from the house with Cado. Lance had had hardly any time off since they had set up the company. It was time he had at least today off. He held Cado and headed to the wood with Gwyn by his side. They were to visit Avalon and then venture out onto the open hillside. They were in no hurry. They had plenty of time before they went out for dinner this evening.

They sat by the shore of the lake and gazed across at the island. Everything appeared tranquil and calm. It appeared to be exactly as it should. Someone was missing though. The mighty King Arthur wasn't here. Gwyn and Lance both instinctively knew he had left them. They looked at each other, and then Gwyn smiled quietly.

"I have a feeling he's been up to some kind of mischief," she said.

Lance gazed at her then looked back at the island. He could only assume that King Arthur had decided to seek revenge for Cindy's suggestion, and he had chosen her wedding day upon which to do so.

Gwyn suspected that this was just the beginning. She envisaged the king treating Cindy in exactly the same way in which she had treated Lance. She suspected that Cindy would lose her credibility slowly, unless events changed Arthur's plans. It would be best for them to stand back and let Arthur play his game. Gwyn was sure Cindy would deserve everything that was coming to her.

Lance suddenly felt as though it wasn't right as he looked down at Cado. He had a beautiful wife and a young son. He also had a house of his own in a place he never wanted to leave. He wasn't seeking revenge for everything Cindy had said and done. He had something she would never have. He had discovered what true happiness really was. The naturally beautiful woman beside him was giving him that. With Gwyn by his side, he wanted for nothing.

Cindy, however, had committed the most heinous of crimes. She had cast aspersions on Arthur and Guinevere. This wasn't about what she had said about Gwyn and Lance. This was about what she had suggested about Arthur and Guinevere. That was what was unforgivable. That was why Cindy had to be punished. They could do nothing to stop this punishment from being given. Arthur, in reality, had no choice. He had to seek retribution for Cindy's remarks and claims. What he was going to do would, in time, be revealed to them.

Lance silently scolded himself. He wasn't supposed to be thinking about Cindy. Today was supposed to be about him and his two companions. King Arthur had decided to make his move today, and there was nothing he could do about it. He decided it was best for them to head up onto the hills so he could take his mind off what was happening.

Gwyn stood up and waited patiently for him to join her. He didn't want to spend the whole day fretting over what

Arthur had planned to do to Cindy. He didn't want to let it spoil this time they had together. His wife should rightfully be the focus of his attention. He didn't want Cindy to win through him thinking about her instead. He needed to clear all thoughts of her out of his head.

They left the trees and headed away across the hills. The day was a warm summer's day, and the pair wandered casually across the open hillside. There was colour everywhere with the multitude of flowers breaking up the carpet of grass and softening the uniform green that would otherwise dominate the landscape. They were in no hurry. They instead wanted to take everything in. They had all of this on their doorstep—this open expanse of clear air and rolling hillside. It proved more than enough to banish all thoughts of Cindy Peterson from their minds.

They eventually returned home late in the afternoon. They hesitated at the edge of the trees before they stepped into the yard. A whole host of people swarmed around in front of them. Their computer equipment was being carried out of the office and loaded into a small white van. Lance stared at the scene as Rick quickly joined them.

"What's going on?" Lance asked.

Rick tried his best to sound off-hand and not the least bit bothered as he explained.

"Both your father's and Jim Peterson's companies have been effectively shut down by some virus. Neither of them can operate at the moment."

"So why is our equipment being seized and taken away?"

Rick hesitated before answering.

"Cindy's claimed we're responsible for the attack."

Lance predictably reacted quickly and voiced his objection. Rick tried to remain rational and calm.

"There's nothing to worry about," he said. "As soon as the origin of the virus has been tracked, everyone will see you had nothing to do with it."

"What do you mean by everyone will see I had nothing to do with it?"

Rick hesitated again. He was obviously reluctant to say anything more. He then sighed and gave in.

"She's blaming you. She's made a personal attack on you. She's claiming you've done it out of spite for losing your inheritance. She's said you've deliberately spoiled her wedding day. She'll realise her mistake when the source of the outbreak has been identified. In the meantime, it means we're also out of action. We'll hopefully get everything back by this time tomorrow."

"But I haven't done anything."

"We all know that, Lance, but the police do have to investigate the allegation."

"Maybe they should take Lance's personal laptop too," Gwyn suggested. "We have nothing to hide."

Lance could do nothing but stand back and watch as everything was taken away. There had to be some mistake. This couldn't be happening. He went cold as Cindy's threat to bring them down echoed in his mind. He would never do something like this though. He would never stoop to her level.

Gwyn ushered him into the house as the police drove away. She wanted to get Cado fed, bathed and in his cot before they got ready to go out for dinner. Lance reluctantly headed indoors. The others were locking the office and going home. They could do nothing until they got their equipment back.

Gwyn was wearing her black dress when she walked into the living room. Lance immediately recognised it as the one she had worn when she had first stayed with him all night. All thoughts of Cindy were gone. He wasn't going to be able to concentrate on his meal this evening. They climbed into the car and drove to a secluded restaurant. He couldn't focus on the meal he was eating. She was distracting him too much. He just wanted this meal to come to an end and get her home.

Chapter Twenty-Two

Lance was sitting in the office with Cado perched on his lap. Their computers had been seized four days ago and Rick had, through frustration, bought a new computer so they could at least deal with the orders made. Gwyn, Nancy and David had gone to visit Laura and Becky in the shop in Glastonbury, leaving Lance to care for Cado. They had been gone for hours now, not that Lance cared. He couldn't do much, not without his computer.

Anna was packaging up some orders and Rick and Will were deep in conversation. Lance wasn't taking much notice of what was going on around him. He was focusing instead on his son as the toddler bit on a toy in an attempt to relieve his teething pain. The background noise of the conversation suddenly stopped as Rick looked out of the window and cursed.

"What on earth does he want now? Your father's here, Lance. You stay right there."

Lance watched him slip outside then looked across at Will and Anna. He knew why his father had travelled over here from America. It didn't take a genius to work out the reason. They could do without this intrusion at the moment, even though it was inevitable it would happen. Will and Anna crossed over to the window and watched the confrontation between Rick and Blake. Will then suddenly cursed mildly, and his cursing made Lance look at him again. Blake was heading towards the office.

Lance remained seated on his chair. He looked up when the door burst open and Blake stepped inside. He tightened his hold a little as Cado jumped. Blake quickly looked around the room and focused on Lance. He glared at him and hesitated for the briefest of moments when he looked at Cado. Lance was holding and caring for his own son in a way he himself had been denied. Blake had never bothered about him in this way. This was an experience they had both missed out on. Blake stared at Cado before he looked back at Lance and reverted back to his old self in an instant.

"What the hell do you think you're doing?" he demanded. "What kind of cheap stunt was that, contaminating us with that virus?"

Lance's eyes remained on his father as Rick stepped back into the room. He remained calm and quiet as Arthur's presence filled the office.

"We've done nothing, sir."

"Oh don't give me that! We don't believe you for a moment. You've completely ruined our wedding day. Cindy was really looking forward to it, but then you wrecked it in such a vindictive way. She's inconsolable and completely distraught."

Arthur's influence helped Lance to remain calm and confident.

"We had nothing to do with it, sir."

Rick looked round as a small white van pulled up outside. It had distracted him when he was about to speak. Blake continued with his tirade. He stopped only when the newcomer appeared alongside him and showed his ID card to him.

"I'm DCI Collins. I've brought your equipment back with my apologies for us keeping it for so long. We've finished our investigation now."

"When are you going to bring criminal charges against the culprit?" Blake questioned.

He stared directly at Lance as his hostility clearly showed in his eyes. The detective followed his gaze and then looked back at Blake again.

"We'll not be charging anyone," he informed. "I expect our colleagues in America will do though. The source of the virus that's crippled both companies has been traced to a computer in your offices in Boston—to the computer in your own office in fact."

Lance had been watching Cado. He now looked up sharply at Blake and the detective. Blake was momentarily lost for words. A ridiculous suggestion had just been made.

"That's not possible," he objected. "Only Cindy and I know the password to my computer. We were nowhere near the office when everything went down."

"You didn't need to be, sir," the detective pointed out. "The virus could have been sent at any time between everything being shut down the day before and it all being started up that morning. The starting up was all that the virus needed to take a hold. It was simple enough to do, if the person knew how to access every computer that's been infected."

"I couldn't have possibly done it," Blake insisted. "I don't know how to access Jim Peterson's computers."

Maybe it was King Arthur's presence giving him confidence, but Rick couldn't stop himself from blurting out his comment.

"Cindy would know."

He automatically stepped back a little as Blake glared at him.

"Why would Cindy do something like that, on her wedding day of all days too?"

"Perhaps we should invite her in so we can ask her," Rick suggested.

"She's not here. She's stayed in Boston. She didn't want to see any of you after what Lance…"

Blake stopped momentarily as he looked at the detective.

"One of them must've gone to Boston," he claimed. "Lance knows how to access my computer. He had time to get back here before anyone would've known what he'd done."

"What kind of accusation is that to make against your own son?"

Blake stared at the sadness in Rick's eyes and then glared at Lance.

"He's no son of mine," he stated. "He's behind this virus. I just know he is. I don't know how, but I know he's guilty."

"He hasn't been out of this country for months, sir," the detective informed. "According to the checks we've made over the last few days, the last time he was away was to attend a court hearing in Boston last summer, for a paternity lawsuit made against him. I can categorically confirm that no one who works here has been to America in this time-frame. Besides, as you've just said yourself, only you and your wife know the password to access your computer. It appears the finger of blame is pointing towards either you or your wife."

"I wouldn't dream of doing such a thing."

"Well that leaves only one possible suspect," Rick pointed out. "It's time for you to leave. Why don't you go home and ask Cindy? We have work to do, so we can catch up with our workload after we've been inconvenienced in this way. So unless you intend to at least apologise for your accusations… after all, it ruined Lance and Gwyn's first wedding anniversary too."

Blake glared at them with his mouth set in a hard line. He then turned and marched out of the office. He slammed the car door shut once he had climbed in and was quickly gone. Lance watched the car disappear. He knew Blake would be livid. He hated being shown up like this. Cindy had made the accusations though. She had pointed her finger at him. Rick appeared beside him.

"You could claim compensation. We've been inconvenienced with having our equipment seized. And then there's the personal attack on you…"

Lance barely glanced at him as he shook his head. He wasn't looking for compensation. They hadn't lost any trade, despite the inconvenience. He'd have been surprised if Cindy hadn't blamed him. There was nothing to say she was the guilty person. She could have paid any number of people to do it. She only needed to give them the required information. She would've ensured there was no chance of tracing it back to her.

"We should be unloading our things," he said. "Detective Collins has been kind, bringing it over and letting us know what happened. We shouldn't be holding him up."

Rick, Will and Anna hesitated then fetched their equipment while the detective stayed with Lance.

"He's right you know," the detective told him. "You could sue for slander at the very least."

"What would that achieve? My father's disowned me, if you hadn't gathered. Not that he's been much of a father. I'm far better off without him. I don't want to be like him, and I don't want to take any action against him or Cindy."

"Is this likely to happen again?"

Lance glanced at him.

"Most probably, yes."

He hesitated then reluctantly explained.

"Your ex fiancée has married your father?"

"A year after I was supposed to marry her, yes. He refuses to believe she's only after his company though. We managed to get out before she could do anything to us for exposing her. She's been trying to get a reaction ever since, but I'm not going to give her the satisfaction."

"She'll be expecting a claim for compensation."

Rick was plugging in one of the computers, and he was too busy watching what he was doing to look round.

"I know, which is why we're not going to make one."

The detective said nothing as he looked at them all. He decided to leave now the van was unloaded. He was eager to get back to his office and research this case. There was more going on than he had been told, of that he was certain. He climbed into the van and waited for the approaching car to clear the drive before leaving.

Gwyn, Nancy and David watched the van disappear away before they joined the others in the office. Will was setting everything up as Gwyn crossed over to Lance. Something had happened, and she wanted to know what.

"My father's just visited. He's here without Cindy. The detective turned up and told us the source of the virus has been traced to the computer in my father's office in Boston."

"You mean Blake was behind it?" Nancy looked shocked.

"I don't think he was," Rick spoke up. "Only he and Cindy know the new password to his computer, and he doesn't know how to access Jim Peterson's computers."

"So it must have been Cindy," Nancy nodded knowingly.

"I'm not so sure," Lance said quietly. "King Arthur wasn't here at the time. It's lucky you weren't here, David. I'm sure my father would've accused you if you were."

David had a direct link to Blake's company, and a reason to seek vengeance. It was something that Blake hadn't yet considered. Relations were already bad enough without his father remembering the connection. For now, it was best for things to be left exactly as they were.

Chapter Twenty-Three

Lance needed to speak to King Arthur. He needed to know whether he was responsible for the computer virus. He let Gwyn take Cado as they headed across to the wood and disappeared among the trees. Blake's visit had surprised him, despite it being expected. Lance hadn't expected him to come alone though. He had never known Cindy pass up the opportunity to watch him squirm. He could only assume she must have had an ulterior motive to stay in Boston.

King Arthur and Guinevere were waiting for them on the shores of the lake. Someone else was standing beside them. Gwyn recognised King Leodegrance immediately. He was reunited with his daughter and son-in-law again. Lance didn't need introducing to this newcomer. King Leodegrance had already been mentioned and his return predicted. They bowed out of habit and respect as they greeted each other.

"We've watched and heard everything that was spoken just now," Arthur said, "and your father could have, at the very least, apologised for the accusations he made."

Blake Brookes never apologised for anything, and Lance wasn't looking for or expecting one. There was really only the one thing he needed to know. Arthur smiled kindly.

"I'm not the one responsible for the computer virus. I did go to Boston with the intention of doing something. Someone else was there and already at work though. He had been shown how to shut off the alarms and security cameras. He was finishing what he was doing when I arrived. He left no trace of his presence. He was careful not to leave any prints."

"It wasn't Cindy?" Lance sounded surprised.

"She didn't actually carry out the deed," Arthur confirmed. "She did, however, write down the information her lover needed. Yes, Phil Jameson is the one who actually went in and committed the crime, with Cindy's help. They met up afterwards and burned the written instructions to dispose of the evidence. He is also the reason why she isn't here now. She wants to spend this time with him in your father's house. Your father can't argue against the evidence you've been given. Their investigation had proved the source of the virus and that you were here at the time. It's all turned out better than I'd planned. Your father has a lot to think about. He's beginning to realise what a big mistake he's made."

Lance stared into space and then looked back up at the mighty king. Arthur smiled down at him.

"I believe your father won't return here again. He has lost face, and has had a fool made out of him. He's starting to come to his senses, and is going to ask some awkward questions. His young wife will realise, once again, she's not as clever as she believes. She's still confident at the moment though. She believes she still has the upper hand. It's all contributing to her ultimate downfall. You have enough to think about already to keep your mind occupied. We'll deal with the little lady. We want and need you to just concentrate upon what you have here. Right here is where you're needed at the moment."

"It's time for you to return home," Guinevere spoke up. "Your mother is incensed by the treatment you've received from your father. It won't be wise to allow her to phone your father."

Lance gazed at her as her words sank into his brain. He could easily imagine what his mother would say if she did make that call, as Guinevere had said. They weren't supposed to be retaliating. They needed to remain quiet and keep their dignity. Lance and Gwyn bowed slightly, backed away and then turned and made their way back through the trees.

Nancy and David were talking to Rick, Will and Anna. They had been told what had happened, and Nancy was indeed incensed enough to want to phone Blake. He had over-stepped the mark and gone too far. She pulled out her mobile phone. Lance didn't want her to make that call though. Nancy stared at him in disbelief.

121

"I know it was wrong of my father to make those accusations, but he now knows we had nothing to do with the virus that has brought both companies to a standstill. He also knows we've been inconvenienced by Cindy blaming me. He has to know we could justifiably put in a claim for compensation for the wrongful accusations. If we do or say anything though then we'll only achieve making him hate me all the more."

He had to remain quiet and not react to anything. Cindy would have won if he did. He would have lowered himself to her level. He had to remain dignified and have faith in King Arthur ensuring things would turn out right in the end. The mighty king though was not responsible for the computer virus.

"Well it couldn't have been Blake or Cindy," Nancy remarked. "They both had other people with them at the time."

"Cindy got Phil Jameson to do it," Lance informed. "She arranged to have her own wedding sabotaged. She did it for maximum effect and so she could point the finger of blame at me. After all, it would've been possible for me to go over and do it then return here before the virus took a hold. Granted it would have been tight, but it would've been possible. Cindy made two mistakes though. She changed the password to my father's computer and she infected all her father's computers too. She didn't think it through properly. She should've sent Phil to the offices here and just infected my father's computers. It would've really looked as though I'd done it then."

They needed to simply get on with their own work, as though nothing had happened. Cindy would expect some kind of reaction, but he wasn't going to give her that. Blake would be starting to suspect her. He would know he wasn't behind it, and only he and Cindy knew how to access his computer. Lance didn't need to retaliate. Blake would do that. They needed to stand back, watch, wait and see what happened next.

"I'll start getting lunch ready," Gwyn said. "I don't doubt you have a lot of work to catch up on now you have your gear back."

Nancy hesitated. David urged her to leave the group in the office to their work. She begrudgingly followed Gwyn, who had disappeared to change Cado's nappy. She soon returned and sat him in his high chair with a rusk and bottle of milk. Nancy still felt indignant as she made some coffee. She couldn't believe that Lance didn't want her to give Blake a piece of her mind.

Cindy had to have known the source of the virus would be traced. She had made sure it was done when she was surrounded by plenty of people who would verify she was nowhere near the building. She had made it look as though Blake was the culprit. Blake knew he had nothing to do with it. It was easy when they could point their fingers at Lance. They couldn't do that now, and Blake knew Cindy couldn't have done it. Only someone who knew how to turn off the alarms and security cameras, access that particular computer and access the computers of both companies could have done it.

"I expect Lance's father will be trying to work out who could've done it," Gwyn said. "I don't doubt he'll suspect Phil Jameson, but he has no proof. We'll only aggravate things if you have a go at him."

"I guess he'll not take too kindly to that," Nancy confessed. "There's still no excuse for him not apologising to Lance for his accusations. He should at least swallow his pride and do that."

Blake would never do that though. He wasn't the type of person who apologised for anything. He would only grow increasingly irate with Nancy and shout obscenities at her if she did phone him. Gwyn suspected that was exactly what Cindy wanted. She would want to keep a rift between them. She wouldn't want Blake to return to them. She needed him to feel isolated to ensure she got everything he owned. She wanted a reaction. She wanted them to retaliate. She would be incensed by them doing nothing. Gwyn didn't doubt her trying something else in order to get a reaction. She would grow bolder until she made a mistake and revealed her true intentions. Blake would have hopefully realised what she was doing by then. He would be more willing to come back to them if he wasn't reprimanded or reminded they had tried to warn him.

"Cindy's already made a huge mistake," Gwyn informed. "She cast doubt upon Lance being Cado's father. By accusing me of infidelity, she's also attacked Arthur and Guinevere. They'll not let her go unpunished. They need us to trust them. We need to remain quiet, dignified and strong while they deal out the appropriate punishment. Cindy's downfall will come, and I believe it'll be sooner rather than later. They don't let such accusations drag on for too long. They like to deal with things then move on. She's starting to take chances by sending Lance's father here while she entertains Phil Jameson in his house. She's growing increasingly bold and confident, and that leads to carelessness. She'll get caught out, and it'd be best if we played no part in it. It's best left to Arthur and Guinevere."

Nancy reluctantly agreed to give no reaction. It went against everything she normally did. Gwyn was confident it would all turn out for the best. She knew the most about Arthur and Guinevere. They could only hope she was right.

Chapter Twenty-Four

Gwyn looked out of the window and watched as Lance stopped his car in the yard. He had returned from taking Nancy and David to the airport. He looked across at the house and hesitated. Rick had appeared in the office doorway and made Lance look at him. He looked reluctant as he walked from his car to the office.

Gwyn smiled knowingly as she turned away from the bedroom window. Cado was having his early afternoon nap. She had pounced on this chance to clean the guest bedroom and main bathroom. They had the house to themselves again, and she wanted to get this cleaning done and out of the way. They could revert back to their own routine and do as they pleased. They could relax. The past few days had been far from easy with all the accusations made.

She picked up the dirty linen and made her way down to the kitchen. She was loading the washing machine when the door opened. She looked up and watched as Lance let himself into the room. He switched on the kettle and spooned sugar and coffee into five mugs while Gwyn switched on the washing machine. Lance kept his eyes on the coffee and sugar as he spoke.

"I met Graham at the airport. He'd just dropped my father off when I came out of the terminal. I don't know how I missed him, but I'm glad I did. Graham was really embarrassed. He kept apologising for everything that's happened lately. I told him we know it's got nothing to do with the staff. I told him we know it's my father and Cindy behind everything, and especially Cindy."

"It sounds as though it was quite an awkward meeting," Gwyn remarked.

"It was to begin with. He was happy to talk though. He said my father's been furious ever since he learned where the virus came from. He phoned Cindy as they were leaving here.

Graham said he really went for her, and he was frustrated by not being able to get an earlier flight. At least he's not on the same flight as mom and David. I got the impression all hell's going to break loose when my father gets back home. I'm sure Cindy will get away with it though. She's bound to find someone else to blame. She always does. If it means my father starts to suspect her though…"

He wasn't sure he really cared about what was about to happen, and he wasn't sure whether that was an awful thing to say.

"No it's not awful," Gwyn told him. "Not when you consider the life your father's given you. You've managed to move on and start out on your own. You're showing everyone what you can really do."

Lance glanced at her. He preferred to watch the boiling water he was pouring into the mugs.

"Rick's just told me we've been contacted by the chief executive of the Cosmopolitan Hotel group. He wants to see if we can develop a system to use throughout their entire network. He's invited us to their London headquarters to show him what we can do. Rick's arranged a meeting for next Monday. I don't know why they need me there though. Will's developing the business programmes."

"You're in partnership. It has to be a joint decision between all three of you. I'm sure you'll enjoy the trip really."

Lance put the kettle down and took the milk out of the fridge.

"No I won't."

He was determined not to enjoy it. He wanted to stay here with Gwyn and Cado. Gwyn smiled as she watched him finish making the coffee. He hadn't wanted to come to this country two years ago. He had been just as determined then to hate it here. He was now married to her and had permission to live here permanently. She knew he wouldn't want to be reminded of that though. He needed to go to London and admit to himself it wasn't so bad.

The door opened again. Lance said nothing more as the other three joined them. Rick and Will were full of excitement and anticipation. They were obviously looking forward to their day in London. This could be a major breakthrough which went on to bring in many more similar orders. They were taking the train to London and being picked up by a car at the railway station. They were being given a guided tour of the Mayfair Hotel before being treated to lunch there.

"This chief executive must be genuinely serious about us developing a global system for them," Rick enthused. "That'll really make your father sit up and take notice Lance."

Lance gazed at him across the table.

"It'll certainly make Cindy take notice. She's not going to like it one bit."

Rick shrugged his shoulders.

"It's called business. It's what we do. Your father was offered the opportunity to develop Will's software. He chose to turn it down without even looking at it. We decided to take this chance, and hopefully we're going to reap the rewards. We need to show a united front, Lance. We need to show solidarity. All three of us really need to go to London for this meeting. We need you by our side."

"It's only for the day," Gwyn said, "you'll be back here by evening. I want you to show Cindy what you can really do."

"What Will can do you mean."

"Oh come on, Lance!" Will objected. "You know I couldn't have developed this software without either your financial backing or Rick's contacts to help me. Besides, your software is outselling mine by miles. The orders prove that. There's no guarantee the Cosmopolitan group will choose my software. They could still go with someone else's instead. They've only expressed an interest so far. This isn't a definite sale. I say we should just go along, enjoy the day and not expect too much to come of it."

Lance didn't answer. Gwyn smiled knowingly at Rick and Will. He was just suffering an attack of nerves and doubting himself again. There was plenty of time to convince him otherwise before Monday dawned. He didn't have to say anything when they met this executive. He could let Rick and Will do all the talking. There was the possibility that, if their software was accepted there and then, they would need his signature on a contract. They needed him there for that one reason alone.

Lance reluctantly conceded defeat. He would go to London with Rick and Will on Monday. He had no real choice but to do so. He would be glad when it was all over.

Gwyn let herself into the office and handed a mug of coffee to Anna before closing the door again. Lance had left early this morning. He had met Rick and Will at the railway station in Bristol before they had boarded a train for London. They wouldn't be back for hours yet. It was a new experience for all of them and, if nothing else, they would learn from it.

Anna wasn't quite ready to go to the village, despite the stack of small packages on one of the tables. Anna and Gwyn enjoyed this ritual of walking to the store in the village. Cado, as usual, was asleep by the time they reached the shop. The air felt hot and the lane was dusty, but compared to the city, it was clean and fresh.

Gwyn and Anna were soon heading back towards the house again. It was an opportunity for Anna to look at the houses as she walked by. They soon reached the drive and relaxed as they left the traffic behind and walked side by side in the shade of the trees separating the drive from the lane.

"How do you think the guys will get on?" Anna asked. "Will said that, if they're successful, they're going to award themselves a big bonus. I can't help but wonder if we'll be able to buy a house here in the village then. I know I shouldn't get my hopes up too much, but I can't help it."

"Well we can either wait for the men to return or we can go and see Arthur and Guinevere."

Anna slowed as she looked at Gwyn. She did want to know either way but, if it was disappointing news… she was sure she preferred to wait until this evening so she could keep her dream alive for that little bit longer.

"Do you remember what Arthur said?" Gwyn asked. "You're destined to be bigger than Lance's fathers company. It's your reward for believing in Arthur and Guinevere. I believe you'll get your dream home, regardless of whether this hotel chain accepts your software or not. I understand it'll be a huge disappointment if this falls through, but then who knows? It might stop you from buying the wrong house."

Anna gazed at her. She didn't understand. How could her dream home be the wrong house? Gwyn smiled and led Anna into the wood. Guinevere was waiting for them on the shores of the lake. Anna wasn't sure she could ever get used to the uncanny resemblance shared by Gwyn and Guinevere. Guinevere was looking directly at Anna.

"The house you're admiring most isn't your dream home," she warned. "It would be your worst nightmare. You should look further afield instead of focusing on the village. Can you really forsake the convenience of the city and live somewhere so isolated? You are destined to live the life you crave. You only need to believe."

How could Anna not believe? Guinevere smiled warmly as she gazed at the infant sleeping peacefully in the pram.

"Forgive me for asking," Anna said, "but am I right to believe you and Gwyn are related?"

"Gwyn is a descendent of our bloodline yes," Guinevere confirmed.

"I knew it! You look so alike, it's so easy to mistake you for each other."

Guinevere smiled yet again. Anna had shown she really did believe in them, and that was all she needed to do. Maybe, just maybe, then men would return with welcome news.

Chapter Twenty-Five

Gwyn checked the time and stood up. She picked Cado up and carried him through to the kitchen so she could switch on the kettle. Nancy had flown over from Boston and phoned when she was off the aeroplane and in the terminal. She had offered to get a taxi, but Lance had grabbed his car keys so he could go and pick her up. His mother had never arrived unannounced like this before, so they could only assume that something awful had happened.

Gwyn looked out of the window then spooned coffee and sugar into three mugs as the kettle came to the boil. It was late in September, and the heat of the summer was beginning to give way to the cooler temperature of autumn. The trees and hedgerows were still green while the number of ramblers crossing the nearby hills hadn't yet diminished. They were the people without school-aged children who preferred venturing out when the crowds were gone but the weather was still fine. Only the hardiest and most dedicated would be seen in another month or two.

Gwyn looked out of the window again. She knew Lance could return at any moment now. Their driveway, however, was quiet and empty. A sudden flash of light from sunlight reflecting off glass caught her eye as she looked away. A car had turned onto their drive and was heading towards the house. Maybe they could now discover the reason behind Nancy's unexpected visit. Gwyn poured boiling water into the mugs and looked round when the door opened.

Nancy stepped inside and greeted Gwyn in her usual manner. She sounded nervous though, as though she wasn't relishing the prospect of explaining her presence. Lance followed her indoors and glanced at Gwyn as he closed the door behind him. His mother had already avoided telling him why she was here. Gwyn led the way to the living room. She put Cado back down onto the floor and gave him a bottle of milk as she sat on the settee.

"I'm so thrilled to hear I'm to become a grandmother for a second time," Nancy said, "and it's awesome you've been awarded the contract for the Cosmopolitan Hotel chain. That's one in the eye for Cindy. She's insanely jealous. She hates everyone commenting about your success. She's certainly starting to look incredibly stupid after everything she's said about you."

Lance grew increasingly impatient. He knew she was avoiding telling them the reason why she was here, but he wanted to know what that reason was.

"Mom, what's happened to make you go to all the expense and time to come here? What's so bad you can't tell me on the phone?"

Nancy gazed silently at him for a few long moments.

"Oh, Lance, there's no easy way to tell you. Blake came to see me a few days ago. He's finally realised what's going on. Cindy's told him she's pregnant by him, but this time we know for a fact she's lying. Blake and I both know how false her claim is this time. It's all going to become very public soon. He wants me to tell you the truth before everyone else finds out."

Lance was frustrated. He didn't understand what she was trying to say.

"What are you telling me, mom? How can you be so certain this time?"

"This is so awkward and embarrassing. I really don't know how to say this."

She glanced up to find Lance staring at her. She couldn't meet his gaze as she took a deep breath.

"Blake's actually not your father. We found out years ago that he's infertile. He's had tests and everything done to prove he can't have children. He was absolutely devastated. He so desperately wanted a son and heir. He'd just set up his company at the time. He and David got on so well back then…"

Lance looked stunned as he stared into space.

"I'm so sorry, Lance. We never meant for anyone to find out. No one needed to know. Then your... Blake stupidly married that Cindy Peterson. You know what he's like. He'll not keep quiet about this. He'll confront her sooner or later, and probably sooner. He wants you to know before he does so you're ready for what'll happen. That's why he asked me to come and tell you."

"Who is my real father?" Lance asked quietly.

"David," Nancy informed. "It was Blake's idea. He really wanted a child to call his own, but he refused to adopt. He didn't want anyone else to know he can't have children. He couldn't face the shame. He kept on at me and David to... well, you know. We didn't want to, and it was only supposed to be until I was expecting you. We'd grown very close to one another by then though, which is why Blake fired David. He hadn't liked the way we carried on seeing each other. I really am sorry, Lance. We never set out to hurt anyone. It was supposed to have been a secret between just us three."

David Whealdon was his real father? A lot of things were suddenly very clear. Lance now understood why David showed such an interest in him. It explained why he so desperately wanted to be accepted by him. When Blake had denounced him as his son he had been telling the truth.

"I'm truly sorry about having to tell you all this, Lance. I know it sounds so sordid and unsavoury, but it wasn't like that. It was because you were wanted so badly. Blake thought it'd be much easier and more convenient, and it meant very few people knowing he can't father any children. If you don't want to see David again, then he's prepared to stay away."

Lance looked sharply at Nancy then gazed into space again. He wasn't ready to say anything just yet. He didn't know whether he still wanted David in his life. He had started to accept him as his step-father, and he now faced being asked to accept him as his natural father. How was he supposed to react towards the man he had believed to be his father? He knew Blake wouldn't be able to stop himself from confronting Cindy over her claim. It would be impossible for him not to.

Blake was also being a coward. He didn't know how Lance would react to this revelation. He couldn't face him, so he had sent Nancy here to tell him instead. Blake had said and done so many things lately that he feared Lance's reaction.

"He's already changed his will, Lance. The lawyers are holding it for safe-keeping. He's given me a copy to hand to you. He wants to make sure Cindy gets nothing. He's leaving everything to you…"

"I can't…"

"He wants you to have everything, Lance. It's the only way he knows to make it up to you. He's really ashamed of the way he's treated you believe it or not. He believes something awful is going to happen to him when he confronts Cindy. He's certainly expecting to suffer an unfortunate and fatal accident. He's seen and acknowledged what you're capable of achieving. He needs to know he's leaving everything in safe hands. He believes it'll be far safer in your hands."

Lance didn't know what to do. He needed time to think about it. He needed to go to Avalon to seek Arthur and Guinevere's wisdom and guidance. Nancy watched him disappear then eventually looked at Gwyn, who smiled sympathetically.

"That couldn't have been easy for you, having to tell Lance that," she said.

"It wasn't. I can't blame him if he hates us all for what we've done."

"I don't think he'll do that. You will stay won't you? I'd best go and see how he is. I'd hate you to leave before we come back."

She picked Cado up and followed Lance into the wood. She soon joined him, Arthur and Guinevere on the shores of the lake. Lance looked disappointed when told his mother was still here. His mind span wildly and he wasn't sure he could face her. It was all such a mess. It did explain why he had never been able to connect with his… Blake. Cindy was going to get an enormous shock when she found out. He didn't want to think about her probable reaction though. He didn't want to see his father getting hurt, despite the way he had always treated him.

"How your father deals with this is for him to decide," Arthur stated. "You can't do that for him. You do have a decision of your own to make, however."

Lance gazed up at Arthur then swallowed as he looked away again. He had his own company here now, and they were proving to be as successful as Arthur and Guinevere had predicted. He couldn't manage both companies, and he didn't want to have to give up what he had here. All the people employed at his father's Bristol offices though…

"Why don't you talk it through with the others?" Gwyn suggested. "Why don't you discuss all the options you have? You never know, you might find owning your father's company could benefit your one here. Maybe you should talk it through with Rick and Will. Your father wants to ensure Cindy gets nothing more from him. I don't doubt he wants to make sure she's punished properly for everything she's done. I even suspect your father is seeking your blessing before he says anything to her. He obviously wants it all sorted before he does. It all depends upon whether you can forgive him for what he's done."

Lance looked from Gwyn to Arthur and Guinevere then back at Gwyn again. He knew that if anything happened to Blake, he would always regret not trying to make peace with him. That was what all of this was about—remaining dignified and not retaliating. He was numb with shock while still in turmoil. He had no real choice but to forgive them all for what had happened. No one was pretending it was going to be easy, but publicly he knew they had to show a united front. He had no other choice if Cindy was to be punished for her allegations against Arthur and Guinevere.

Chapter Twenty-Six

Lance sat on the shore and gazed at the island at the centre of the lake. Gwyn was beside him while Cado played quietly with one of his toys. Gwyn kept a watchful eye on their son. She knew Lance would speak sooner or later. He had just returned from taking Nancy to the airport after a two-day stay. He hadn't said much in that time, and there was no knowing what he was thinking. Gwyn knew, however, that the revelation was constantly playing on his mind.

"Why has this happened?" Lance asked. "Why do I have a different father to the one I believed to be all my life? I understand that no one wanted to deliberately upset me, and that they believed only they needed to know, but why does it have to be me? I'm still trying to grasp the fact I have a different father. I hate to admit I feel closer to David than my father, or the man I thought was my father. Everything's just got complicated."

"How complicated do you want it to be? At the end of the day, you're here because you were desperately wanted."

Lance glanced at her then at Cado then Avalon and then at the ground in front of his feet.

"What would my life have been like if David and not my... Blake had been my father from the very beginning? How can someone give up their own child like that? How can someone force two people together just to create a child? What would I be doing now if mom and David had raised me?"

Lance knew the answers without needing to be told. He would have never been involved with Cindy if his biological parents had raised him. He wouldn't have been allowed anywhere near her. And he certainly wouldn't now be here with Gwyn. If Blake hadn't taken him in as though he was his own son, then he would have never been sent here to England. He would be living in Boston and he wouldn't have known about her existence. In some warped way, what had happened had brought him here. It had given him the opportunity to be with Gwyn after releasing Arthur from the spell that kept him on Avalon. Could Arthur and Guinevere have planned this from the moment Nancy and David were forced together? Lance looked at Avalon as he heard Guinevere's voice on the breeze.

"Our involvement doesn't go back that far," she said. "Our part only goes back as far as the moment you first came across Avalon. Your real father wasn't born in America. He was born in England and then taken to America when his family emigrated. He was only a small boy at the time. He'll tell you about all of that if it's what you want to know."

Lance didn't know if he did want to hear at the moment. He did know that he did need to speak to Blake, Nancy and David. He needed to meet them face to face and talk to them about this revelation. He suspected that none of them would know what to say, but he needed to find out what had happened. They were the only people who could tell him.

"I'll have to phone them and arrange to meet up. I want that to happen here, in this country. I won't feel welcome or safe in Boston. One of us needs to make the first move, and I guess that has to be me."

He wasn't looking forward to making that move. He knew he couldn't put off doing it though.

"I'm sure they won't mind if you take a few more days to think things through first. It's a lot to take on board and come to terms with. I expect your mum will talk to both your fathers when she gets back home. What about the others in the office? They know that something's happened, but they don't know what. It's been impossible not to notice. You need to get things clear in your own mind before you think about possibly telling other people though. You need to know how you feel about it first."

"I don't know how I feel. The only reason I'm here at all is because my father forced my mother and his work colleague together in his desperation to have a son. He couldn't do that himself. You're right, I am here because I was wanted. I don't know if he'd have treated me any differently if I really was his own son. Only my father can tell me that. I don't know if I do want to know the answer at the moment."

Gwyn said nothing. She let him continue to sit quietly. She understood why he needed to come here. He needed to soak up the calm and tranquil atmosphere so he could begin to make some sense out of what he had been told. He could see why his mother had never really bothered about him. She had been too preoccupied and had preferred to spend her time with David instead of being at home raising and protecting him. He couldn't help but feel angry at being abandoned by his own mother. Maybe he hadn't let anyone down after all. Maybe it had been the other way round.

"I expect my father will confront Cindy as soon as mom's spoken to him," he said suddenly. "I expect everyone will know then. I have to let Rick, Will and Anna know before that happens."

"Would you like me to tell them?" Gwyn offered. "I know it shouldn't be me, but I don't need to go into detail. I only need to tell them you've been told your step-father is really your biological father. There won't be any pressure on you to discuss it in detail then. They'll already know before it goes public so they'll not be shocked. It'll just give you a little more time to come to terms with what you've been told."

"I don't know, Gwyn. It'd be like I'm running away from it, just like I used to run away from everything. Maybe we should go back home so I can invite everyone in for a coffee. I have to face this sooner or later, so I'd just as well do it now and get it over with. There's no point in putting it off any longer. I don't want to say anything about my father having changed his will again yet though. I need to talk to him about everything first before I discuss anything like that with the others. Besides, with the way things have been lately, that could easily change before all of this is over."

He stood up. His mind was made up, and Gwyn wasn't about to argue with him. He needed to tell the others himself, and needed to tell them before it became common knowledge. He couldn't waste any time. He knew his father, and that he would act as soon as his mother had spoken to him. It was only fair the others knew before that happened. Lance didn't want to shy away and be a coward this time.

Rick, Will and Anna stared at Lance in disbelief. They were sat at the kitchen table while Cado sat in his high chair with a rusk and a bottle of milk. Gwyn looked at them occasionally as she made some coffee. She handed the mugs round then sat between Lance and Cado as Rick found his voice.

"We guessed something had happened, but not for a moment did I imagine it'd be something like this."

Lance refused to look at them as he shrugged his shoulders.

"I guess it's not so bad. At least I know now, and I already know David. It explains his eagerness to be accepted by me. I wanted you all to know before my father confronts Cindy. I guess it's not his fault he can't have children, and it's only being revealed now because Cindy's expecting again. There's no denying she had to be cheating this time."

"It must've been an awful shock for you to find this out," Anna said.

"As Gwyn's said, it shows how much I was wanted. If he hadn't assumed the role of my father I wouldn't be here now. None of us would be. I'd have never been with Cindy or sent over here. We wouldn't have needed to leave his company for our own safety. We wouldn't be doing what we're now doing. We wouldn't be now doing our own thing and doing very well out of it too. I guess we could say Cindy's done us a huge favour."

"Even so Lance," Rick remarked, "it's still a massive shock."

Lance wasn't denying that. He couldn't deny it. His mother had thought it best to come over and tell him in person. He still needed time before he could hopefully come to terms with the news. He at least now knew, and it was only fair he told them all before it became public knowledge. He needed to phone both his fathers to arrange meetings so they could talk. He wanted to do that face to face, and not in America. He couldn't just stop looking at Blake as his father because he'd been told otherwise. He had raised him as though he was his own son. They had all believed their actions had been the easiest solution. No one had expected this to happen. It had happened though, and they had been forced to confess. He didn't know what was going to happen now. It all seemed to be a mess that might never get sorted out, which was why he needed to talk to his two fathers. It was the only way to find out where they went from here.

"Maybe once I've talked to them I'll be able to talk to you about it properly. I can't do that just yet. I don't know how I feel about it at the moment. Mom's bound to talk to my father when she gets back home, and you know what he's like. He's guaranteed to go public at the first opportunity."

Lance was still calling Blake his father. He had looked upon him as his father for the whole of his life so far though. It was impossible for him to think otherwise just because he now knew differently. Blake was the one he needed to talk to first, and that much he did know. He needed to know exactly where he stood with Blake before he could face David. Maybe, once this coming weekend was over, he would be able to muster the courage he needed to make that first phone call.

Chapter Twenty-Seven

Lance looked puzzled as he stared at his mobile phone as he switched it off. He couldn't understand why he wasn't getting an answer. It wasn't like his father not to answer his phone like this. He could, after all, be missing an important business deal. Lance instinctively knew something was wrong. He looked at Gwyn then back at his phone and dialled another number. He held the phone against his ear and looked at her again while waiting for the call to be answered. She had settled Cado in his cot for the night. She was now kneeling on the floor as she packed his toys into a large plastic box. Lance gazed at her and was taken by surprise when the call was answered.

"Mom, it's me. I've been trying to phone my father these last couple of days but I'm getting no answer. I'm beginning to feel concerned about him. It's only to arrange to talk to try and find out where we all stand after what you've told me."

Lance paused as he listened carefully to what Nancy said. He then thanked her and switched off his phone again. He gazed into space, as though trying to work something out, before suddenly returning to the here and now. Gwyn was still kneeling on the floor, despite all the toys now stored in the box. She was looking at him, as though patiently and expectantly waiting for an explanation. He made eye contact for a few long moments but couldn't continue to meet her gaze. He crossed over to the settee.

"Mom's going to try and get hold of my father," he informed. "I don't like this. I don't like it one bit. It's not like my father not to answer his phone. He's always answered it as soon as it starts ringing."

Gwyn stood up and joined him on the settee.

"There could be a perfectly reasonable explanation," she said.

"What possible explanation can there be? My father's company is his whole world. It's all he's ever cared about. And mom did warn me he's likely to confront Cindy as soon as he knows that I know the truth. I don't want to think about what she's likely to do, especially if she hears he's changed his will again too. I have this horrible feeling that something awful has happened."

Gwyn took his hand and held it in both of hers.

"You don't know that it has. You're letting your imagination run wild. It's taking a hold of you so you're only able to think irrational thoughts. You've done everything you possibly can. I'm sure your mum will phone as soon as she finds out what's going on."

Lance knew that, annoyingly, she was right. He had done everything he could without actually flying over to Boston. He knew that, at the moment, he was far from welcome over there. He was viewed as the one responsible for causing all the trouble and hatred that had been stirred up lately. There really was nothing else he could do. He could only wait until his mother phoned him, and that would probably take hours. He was unlikely to hear anything before the first rays of morning sunlight reached out from the distant horizon.

He sighed and put his phone down beside the two mugs of coffee he had made while Gwyn had settled Cado. He couldn't shake this feeling that something awful had happened. Maybe, hopefully, it was just his imagination running wild. He could only think of the internet conversations between Cindy and Phil Jameson. He didn't need to read them again to know what had been written. They were etched on his brain and something he would never forget.

Gwyn rubbed his arm gently and sympathetically. She always seemed to know what was on his mind. She always seemed to understand what he was thinking. She didn't need to read every minute detail to guess what Cindy had once planned to do to him. Now she, like Lance, feared that Cindy may have exacted her revenge on Blake Brookes instead.

They both knew it would make no difference to Cindy who actually suffered the fate she already had planned out.

The evening dragged. Lance took his mobile phone to their bedroom when they did eventually retire for the night. There wouldn't be much sleeping tonight. Gwyn climbed into bed and nestled against him. His arms were around her, but she could sense that his mind was miles away. Neither of them could rest until that phone rang and Nancy gave them some information. The fear of missing that phone call prevented them both from sleeping. It was what had driven Lance to do the unthinkable and bring his phone into their bedroom for the first time.

They eventually dozed off. They couldn't stay awake as the night passed quietly into day. The shrill ringing of the telephone woke them. They both jumped and jerked up as they looked about them in a daze. Lance's mind filled as memories immediately flooded back. He snatched up his phone and answered it. Gwyn focused on the bedside clock and figured out it was the middle of the night in Boston. She could tell from the way Lance was speaking that Nancy was giving him the news he hadn't wanted to hear. It sounded very much as though his greatest fear had come true.

Lance stared ahead of him as he switched off his phone and put it back onto the bedside table. He eventually glanced at Gwyn. He really hadn't wanted to hear what his mother had just told him. That was the last thing he had wanted to hear.

"Mom called my father's office," he said. "They told her Cindy told them they were going away for a few days. They'd been told they weren't to be disturbed in any circumstance. Mom phoned the police and insisted they checked my father's apartment and the country house. They found my father in the house. He was tied up and... tied up and abused in the way they'd planned for me. He's been taken to the hospital. He's in a bad way apparently."

He suddenly threw back the duvet and got up. He needed to go to Boston and see his father. Gwyn watched him as he began to dress then moved across to where he was sitting on the edge of the bed. She placed her hands on his shoulders and spoke quietly and calmly.

"Shouldn't you book a flight first?"

Lance glanced at her then stopped what he was doing as her words slowly sank in. He wasn't thinking straight. He was expecting to go to the airport and get straight onto an aeroplane to fly over to Boston. He needed to make a phone call and book a flight. He snatched up his phone and switched it on before he hesitated again. What number did he dial? Who should he contact? His mind raced and stopped him thinking straight.

"Why don't you finish getting dressed then look online?" Gwyn suggested. "Even if it's only for a phone number to ring."

She waited until he had hurried out of the room before getting up, showering and dressing. Cado could be heard in his room. He was ready to get up for his breakfast while oblivious to this latest drama unfolding in Lance's life. He had only met Blake briefly on a couple of occasions. He wouldn't be able to recall the first meeting soon after he was born. He wouldn't understand what had happened, and would undoubtedly not care about what Blake Brookes had just suffered.

Gwyn carried Cado downstairs, sat him in his high chair and gave him a bottle of milk to drink while getting his breakfast ready. She then made some coffee and toast and made her way to the living room. Lance was on his phone and explaining why he needed to fly to Boston as soon as possible. She said nothing and kept back as he made the call. He eventually switched off his phone and put it on the table beside his laptop.

"The earliest flight I can get is six o'clock tomorrow morning. I'm going on my own. I want you and Cado to stay here, where I know you'll both be safe. I don't want you in Boston, especially at the moment."

Lance quickly stopped her when she began to object. He had to go and see his father, and he was going alone.

"I'm not trying to stop you, Lance. I know it's something you need to do. I just want you to promise me you'll be careful. I assume Cindy's been charged with what she's done."

Lance quickly looked away from her.

"Cindy and Phil have disappeared. No one knows where they are at the moment. I'm sure they'll be caught sooner or later. They'll be hunted down until they've been found. I'm still going over to see my father."

Gwyn was quiet for a few long moments.

"Come and have your breakfast," she urged. "I'm not happy about you going, but I'm not going to try and stop you. I understand why you need to go. I can only ask that you don't go anywhere on your own."

"I can't promise that. I can promise to be careful though. I'm expecting a strong police presence."

"Are you going to phone your mum to let her know you're flying over?"

Lance nodded and dared to look at her.

"I'm sorry, but it's something I really need to do."

"I know. Just make sure you come back in one piece. Cado and I need you. Come and have your breakfast. I expect the others will be here soon. They'll need telling."

Lance hesitated then led the way through to the kitchen. Cado was just finishing his breakfast. He had managed to make a mess everywhere within reach around him. Lance did his best to force a smile, despite being burdened with the knowledge of what had become of his father. Cado had no idea of the enormity of what had happened. Lance ate despite not feeling hungry. Rick, Will and Anna would be here soon. They needed to be told about what had happened. He couldn't expect Gwyn to tell them after he had flown to Boston. That wasn't fair on her. He had to tell them, though he wasn't relishing the prospect. The opposite was true. He was dreading it. They knew he'd been trying to phone his father, and he wouldn't be able to concentrate on work. They would know something had happened whether he said anything or not. He was going to have to tell them.

Chapter Twenty-Eight

"But, Lance," Rick objected, "it's not safe for you over there with Cindy still on the loose."

"I have to go, Rick. I need to see my father after mom's told me he's in a really bad way. And if you remember, I was going to talk to my father anyway. I know it was supposed to happen here, but he's now in hospital and isn't well enough to travel."

"What about Gwyn and Cado?"

Lance gazed at him before turning away so he could avoid looking at any of them.

"They're staying here. I don't want them to go to Boston, not with the way things are at the moment. Gwyn understands why I have to go, despite not being happy about it."

Gwyn appeared in the doorway with Cado in her arms.

"It's true," she said. "We all know what could happen. I know none of us are happy about it, but it's something Lance has to do. I'm not going to stand in his way despite how risky it sounds. Don't forget who we have on our side though. I'm going to see Arthur and Guinevere so I can seek their assurance that Lance isn't going to come to any harm. I want them to tell me he's going to return safe and well."

Gwyn handed Cado to Lance. She waited until he had a firm hold on their son before she let him go. She shut the door behind her and made her way across to the wood, where she walked through the shelter of the trees and soon came to the shores of the lake. The mist swirled above the cold, grey water, its depths hidden from sight. The pale green grass was bathed in an eerie white light and felt warm to the touch.

Two people were wandering across the grass when Gwyn emerged from the trees. She stopped abruptly when she stepped out into the open. She gazed at the couple for a moment or two before she recognised them. One was clad in chain-mail, his hair and beard brown in colour. He looked strong and powerful as his eyes flashed a bright blue. There was no denying he made a fearsome adversary. And yet there was a kindness and gentleness in his manner. His companion was as tall and elegant as he was big and strong. She was wearing a pale blue full-length dress that was covered with a dark blue cloak held in place by a silver clasp. Her skin was pale and her long auburn hair cascaded down her back as her equally blue eyes shone with the same brightness as her companion's.

Gwyn smiled as she greeted them warmly and respectfully. The Lady Vivien had left the water at last and, having reverted back to her original form, was now strolling along the shoreline of her former prison on the arm of her husband, Sir Pelleas. They were reunited, and the brightness in their eyes revealed their pleasure in this time they never dared believe would return. They returned Gwyn's greeting, paused and spoke to her before they moved on. A boat drew alongside the nearby shore, and Arthur and Guinevere stepped onto the grass. Gwyn bowed her head slightly and greeted them.

"I suspect you know that Lance is returning to Boston. The man he believed to be his father is in hospital. He feels a need to go and visit him, despite the danger he's putting himself in. The aeroplane's due to leave here at six o'clock tomorrow morning. I need to know he'll return unharmed. I can only assume his father has confronted Cindy and told her he can't have children of his own."

Arthur and Guinevere looked knowingly at each other then looked back at Gwyn. Arthur spoke first.

"Yes, we know what happened. Cindy didn't believe him to begin with. When she did eventually realise he was telling the truth she drugged him so he fell asleep. She and her lover then tied him up so he was defenceless and unable to escape. I won't go into the details of what they did to him. You only need to know that they made their escape when the police arrived."

He paused for a moment as he gazed kindly down at her.

"I'll travel with Lance. I'll ensure no harm will come to him while he's there. He'll be perfectly safe."

Gwyn desperately wanted to believe Arthur's promise. She couldn't stop herself from fearing for Lance's safety while he was in Boston though.

"I'm sorry, but I don't think I'll be able to believe it until he returns home unharmed."

Guinevere smiled sympathetically.

"It's only to be expected that you fear what might happen. Like it or not though, Lance has to go. This is his opportunity to make peace with Blake while he still can. If he doesn't go now, he'll regret it for the rest of his life. Arthur will be by Lance's side at all times. He's promised to shield him from harm, and he does, after all, need him to return as much as you do. We all need him to return. He'll make sure that Lance is safe."

Gwyn mustered a weak smile as she gazed up at him while Guinevere was doing her best to console her.

"I've been in your position on many occasions. I've been left in Camelot while Arthur embarked on his many crusades. It was expected of him in those dark times, and it was our only regret. He wished on so many occasions that he had mustered the courage to stay with me in Camelot. The expectation for action was too great though. Arthur had no choice but to embark on his crusades. Lance now has no choice but to travel to America. There is one thing he needs to do though. There will be an offering for Blake, an offering that'll be Rick's suggestion. Lance needs to take it with him. It'll ensure the outcome we all want."

Gwyn didn't react for a moment or two. She then nodded and bowed her head once more. She then turned away and glided gracefully back in among the trees. The white light continued to shine down onto the lake behind her, its glow not diminishing as she walked away. She was needed back at home so she could persuade Lance to take the right action. She emerged from the trees and headed over to the office.

Lance was still holding Cado as he glanced at her before looking back at Rick.

"I can't believe what you've done. How could you hide that DVD and memory stick in my car? If I'd known those vile things were there…"

"I'm sorry, but I've not had the chance to retrieve them before now. I never meant for them to stay in your car for this long."

Lance continued to stare at him.

"Rick's suggested I take some copies to my father, Gwyn."

She took Cado from him.

"I think you should," she said.

Lance looked round at her sharply as she explained further.

"Guinevere's just told me you need to take something with you that'll ensure everything turns out right. I don't doubt for a moment that Cindy's already destroyed all the copies she's been given. I expect your father regrets handing them over to her. I've a feeling he'll really appreciate getting his hands on another copy to give him more to use against her. I know it's deeply unsavoury, but I think you're meant to take this evidence over with you."

Lance stared at her in surprised disbelief before suddenly turning away. He took a few moments to think about what she had said then looked back at her again.

"Come back indoors with me while copies are made for you to take with you," she urged.

He hesitated then reluctantly followed her out of the office. He wouldn't be able to concentrate on work today anyway. He closed their door once they were in the kitchen. He looked apprehensive, and he certainly wasn't comfortable with the suggestion made. Rick had, to be fair, already confessed to still having a copy. He just hadn't told him where it was. Maybe it was meant to be. If the DVD and memory stick hadn't been hidden in his car then the police would have found them when they had taken everything away. And Guinevere had said there was something he needed to do—a peace offering to his father that was Rick's suggestion. He needed to take it, whether he liked it or not, to ensure that everything turned out right for them.

"If nothing else, Lance, won't you do it for me?" Gwyn pleaded. "You already know I'm not happy about you going. I'm not trying to stop you though. I'll hate every moment you're not here. I'll not be able to stop fearing the worst, even though King Arthur has promised to go with you and protect you."

"I have to go, Gwyn."

He was adamant, but that didn't stop her from fearing for his safety and that he wouldn't come back to them. Cindy was, after all, still out there with Phil Jameson somewhere. Who knew how desperate and dangerous they would be?

"I don't want Cindy taking you away from me, Lance. I can only put my faith into Arthur and Guinevere. They've told me you need to take this offering to your father. There has to be a reason for it. I can only urge you to take it with you and give it to your father."

Lance gazed at her for a few long moments then sighed as he looked away.

"Well, if it'll make you happy…"

"I'll not be happy until you're safely back here again."

Lance slowly looked back at her. She was his life. She was holding their son while another life was slowly forming inside her. What was he thinking, going away and leaving them behind like this? He had to be mad, wanting to go and see the tyrant who had masqueraded as his father for all these years. How could he want to do that instead of staying here?

"I know that you have to go," Gwyn told him, "and I've been given the impression this will be the only chance you'll get to make peace with your father. I've been told you'll always regret it if you don't go now. And Arthur has promised to be with you at all times. He needs you safely back here as much as I do. As much as I hate the thought of you going, I know you have no choice. I can only ask that you come back home as quickly as possible."

"I don't intend staying away for long. I only intend staying away for long enough to visit my father and offer him a hand of peace. Just one visit should be enough. I always intended flying back here before too many people discovered I'm there."

He suddenly just wanted to be back here with the whole saga behind him. He wanted to go over there and get back here to Gwyn.

Chapter Twenty-Nine

Lance was relieved to see his mother waiting for him at the airport. It was just gone ten o'clock in the morning, meaning it was just three o'clock in the afternoon back at home. Gwyn had got up with him early this morning. She had made sure he had the disc and memory stick in his bag before he climbed into the taxi. She had then stood at the front door and watched as the taxi disappeared down their drive.

Nancy put a protective arm around his shoulders and wanted to know where his luggage was. She was disappointed with the small bag he was carrying. He only intended to stay long enough to visit his father. He didn't want to stay for too long. He didn't want too many people finding out he was here. He wanted to return home before that happened.

Nancy gazed sadly at him as she told him everything would be alright. Once everyone found out what had really happened it would all be very different. Lance refused to look at her. He didn't belong here now. He belonged in England, with Gwyn. He only intended to come here to clear the air with… with the man he had believed to be his father. He needed to talk to him to find out what he really thought about all of this. He couldn't shut Blake out completely, not after all of this time. Lance was fully aware that Blake couldn't expect him to not want to get to know his real father though. It only seemed right to talk to Blake first and explain everything so he understood he didn't want to turn his back on him.

Nancy smiled sadly as she led the way out of the terminal and to where she had parked her car. She was taking him to her apartment first to give him the chance to freshen up and have something to eat. She would then take him to the hospital. Lance knew there was no point in arguing. Maybe it would be best for him to hide in his mother's apartment until he caught his flight home again. He hoped very few people would recognise him with his longer hair while he was here. And Arthur, as promised, was here with him. He had sensed the king's presence beside him when he had climbed into the taxi this morning. It was easy for him to feel safe while knowing he had King Arthur shielding him.

He struggled to eat the food Nancy put in front of him then returned to his room. He opened his bag and pulled out a small envelope. He stared at it for a few moments then reluctantly pushed it into the pocket of his fleece jacket. He hoped that everyone back at home was right. He would be glad when this envelope and its contents were in his father's possession.

"Are you ready?"

Nancy had appeared in the doorway. He looked round and nodded. Yes, he was ready.

He quickly climbed into his mother's car. He was again glad of Arthur's presence as they travelled through Boston. He needed the warrior king's protection right now. He needed to feel the shield against the hostility he believed was aimed towards him by those still loyal to the Petersons. He knew the majority of people here were just that. What their reaction would be once the truth was revealed though, no one knew. He had no intention of being here when they found out. He would, by early tomorrow morning, have already boarded a plane and be heading back to England.

He followed his mother into the hospital then hesitated nervously. He wanted to see his father alone. He in fact needed to go in by himself. This was something that was to be between just the two of them. He would tell his mother and real father everything they needed to know afterwards. Nancy hesitated then nodded before she reluctantly disappeared away after she promised to wait in the hospital foyer. He watched her go then stared at the closed door before him. He took a deep breath and plucked up the courage to open that door.

He peered warily into the room to check he had the right one then slipped inside and closed the door behind him. Blake was lying on his side on the bed in the middle of the room, his face clearly battered and bruised. He already had a visitor standing beside him. Lance didn't recognise him as he hesitated then joined them. He couldn't help but stare down at his father. It was almost impossible to take in the injuries he had suffered, the injuries that had once been planned for Lance. Blake stared defiantly back at him. His voice was cold when he spoke.

"You've heard what's happened to me then."

Lance could only nod his head. His father then accused him of coming here to gloat at him.

"No, sir, I haven't come here to do that. I've been trying to phone you, so we could talk."

Blake saw the sadness in his eyes as he gazed down at him.

"I'll always look at you as my father," Lance said. "We can't change the past, and you're the one who raised me. I can even understand why you did it. I'd have never met Gwyn if my upbringing was any different."

Blake's voice softened.

"She's a good woman, Lance. You've done very well for yourself there."

Lance pulled the envelope from his pocket and offered it to Blake.

"I know. Rick lied. He thought you might like a copy. He asked me to bring them over to you."

Blake gazed up at him and managed a weak smile.

"You mean? You have no idea what this means to me. This is Trevor Jones, from the Boston Globe. I want him to look at it and publish everything he sees. Would you mind?"

Lance shrugged his shoulders as he let the journalist take the envelope from him. He wasn't going to object, if that was what his father wanted. He would already be on a flight back home tomorrow morning. He wouldn't be here when the secret was revealed. They had simply wanted him to have these copies to do whatever he wanted with. Blake smiled again as he relaxed a little. He had cursed over and over for stupidly letting Cindy destroy every last copy. He now, thanks to Rick's deceit, had a reason to keep going. He wanted the world to know what Cindy had planned to do to Lance, and what she had done to him instead. He wanted everyone to know exactly what kind of person she was.

Trevor eyed them both. His curiosity had been roused. He had some dark secret in his hands, a secret that Cindy Peterson desperately wanted to keep well hidden. He wanted to know what was hidden, and what Cindy didn't want anyone else to know. He could sense that there was more to be discovered here, but he decided that secret could wait. There was something of great interest right here in his hands. He needed to get back to his office. He could always return for more information.

Lance watched him go and waited until the door was closed before he reluctantly turned back to his father. He really was sorry about what had been done to him. He wouldn't wish it on anyone. Blake believed he deserved it after his recent behaviour. He certainly hadn't expected Lance to come here to see him. Lance gazed sadly at him.

"I had to come. And I mean what I said, about still looking at you as my father. I can't ignore the part you've played. I wanted to see you, and I want you to continue to be a part of my life. It's why I tried phoning you. I don't deny that I need to get to know my real father, but I'm not going to behave as though you don't exist. I can't do that. You'll always be my father, no matter what anyone might say."

Blake caught him by surprise as he sounded overcome with emotion.

"I don't deserve you. I've treated you appallingly, especially these past few months. I forced them to do it, Lance. I made Nancy and David bless me with the son I desperately wanted. It seemed the easiest and most convenient way. They didn't want to, but I made them because I couldn't face the shame of being unable to father a

156

child. I had it all worked out. I didn't expect to be reminded of David every time I looked at you though. It wasn't your fault, but I still blamed you for everything. Now you're showing me what true dignity is by forgiving us so readily for what we did."

"If you hadn't then I wouldn't be here now. I'm not the one having to face the people here. I'll be hundreds of miles away in England."

"Running your own business. You've done really well. You've certainly shown me what you're capable of achieving when given the chance," Blake hesitated. "Did your mother give you a copy of my will? I need you to accept it all. I need to know my company and fortune is in safe hands. I don't want Cindy to get any of it, not after what she's done. I need you to promise you'll accept it all."

Lance gazed at him and eventually nodded as he solemnly promised. Blake smiled. He was stopped from speaking by the door being opened. Lance looked round when seeing his expression change. Lance's stomach lurched uncomfortably and his mind raced as he reached for the alarm button beside the bed. Hands grabbed him then arms wrapped around him to stop him calling for help.

Cindy stopped in front of him and smirked at him while Phil Jameson held him tightly. He was much larger and far more powerful than Lance could ever hope to be. No amount of struggling was going to free him from the vice-like grip Phil had on him. Cindy couldn't stop gloating.

"How convenient, you turning up like this."

Lance was emboldened by Arthur's presence.

"Whatever you're planning to do, you'll not get away with it."

"Oh I'm sure we will," Cindy smirked all the more. "In fact it's so simple I know we'll get away with it. We're going to kill your father, or whoever he's now claiming to be. We'll then plant the evidence to prove you committed the crime. That should nullify this latest will and make sure I still get everything. It's very obliging of you to turn up like this."

"Just get on with it."

Phil sounded impatient as he continued to restrain Lance. Cindy looked at Phil and smirked yet again as she pulled a syringe from her pocket. She drew out the plunger to fill the syringe with air then turned to face Blake.

"This might take a while," she announced. "It all depends how long it takes the air to reach his heart. I'll force your fingers round the syringe Lance so your fingerprints are found. We'll stay and watch Blake die then we'll take you away to deal with you in a way that'll stop you defending yourself. No one will be able to contradict our explanation. You'll be charged with murder and we'll remain free. There's no escape for you this time. You're well and truly trapped."

Chapter Thirty

Gwyn stood by one of the windows in the reception room and stared outside. She had deliberately left the light switched off so she could look out into the darkness a little better. The aeroplane had to have landed just over an hour ago. She was sure Rick had to be here soon. She could only see the darkness softly engulfing the surrounding trees though.

Her stomach tightened every time a set of headlights pierced the night's darkness on the country lane. Every time, however, those lights had continued on along the lane and made her heart sink again. A car turned onto the driveway at last, and its lights illuminated the drive ahead of it. She caught her breath as her heart skipped a beat. She hurried outside and waited impatiently by the garden gate as the car rolled to a halt nearby. She stepped forwards and then quickly stopped again when Lance climbed out of the car. She hesitated as she gazed at him then crossed over to him.

Lance threw his arms around her and clung tightly to her. He wasn't ready to or about to let her go. She rubbed his back with her hands while she told him how sorry she was about what had happened. She was glad to have him back at home, and she was relieved to have him return safely. He continued to cling onto her and hold her tightly against him until she pulled back from him.

Rick was standing nearby with Lance's bag in his hand. He handed it over and retreated so he could make his escape. Gwyn watched the car begin to disappear down the drive then looked back at Lance again. She held his hand as she spoke quietly.

"Come to Avalon. Cado's fast asleep, and he'll be perfectly safe. The Lady Vivien is watching over him."

He appeared a little reluctant. He put his bag down just inside the garden gate though. He wasn't ready to release his grip on her yet. He needed to hold her, touch her, feel her in order to get the reassurance he was indeed back at home. The last couple of days had been traumatic—a living nightmare. He did need to go to Avalon. Everything would at least be real, comforting and familiar again.

They moved away from the house and walked through the trees to the eerie white light shining ahead of them. They soon reached the shores of the lake and gazed across to the island. King Arthur had been true to his word. He had kept his promise and stayed with him at all times until he was safely returned home. Arthur himself would now also be reunited with his queen on the island before them. Lance stared across at it and silently thanked the king before he sat on the grass. Gwyn was by his side, and he kept a firm hold on her as an overwhelming desire to tell her what had happened swept through him.

"Mom met me at the airport and took me to the hospital. I needed to see my father without her, so she waited for me in the foyer. There was a journalist from the local paper with my father when I joined them. He wanted him to have the DVD and memory stick to run an article in the paper about it. I expect it's appeared in the papers this morning. I didn't care though. I knew I'd already be heading back here by the time the first people began to read it."

Gwyn remained silent. He was talking readily and needed no encouragement.

"The journalist was quick to leave us. My father then acknowledged how he'd noticed how successful we've become. He believed his company will be in much safer hands if left to me. He seemed happy when I promised to accept it. I couldn't refuse really, not after seeing the state he was in. He looked awful. We had the chance to say enough to each other before Cindy and Phil joined us."

Lance hesitated. He wasn't sure he wanted to live through the experience again. Gwyn was rubbing his arm though…

"I tried to call for help, but Phil was too quick for me. I couldn't do anything. I couldn't break free from his grip. I really did try, but… Cindy had brought a syringe with her.

She'd already planned to kill my father. She quickly figured out how she could blame me for the murder so she could claim everything my father owned."

Lance swallowed. He really had tried to free himself from Phil's grip and stop Cindy. Phil was far too strong for him though.

"All these people then burst into the room and grabbed Cindy and Phil, but it was too late. She had already injected air into my father's bloodstream. The medics ran around as they tried to work out how to save my father while Cindy screamed and shouted. She was blaming me. The police took her and Phil away. They left me standing next to my father. I could only wait for him to die. He didn't seem to care. He just kept telling me it'll make things easier for me. He thought he'd only get in the way of me getting to know my real father. Then he was gone, and there was nothing anyone could do to stop it from happening."

"Your father was in a lot of pain, Lance."

He quickly looked up. He hadn't noticed Arthur and Guinevere joining them. Guinevere had spoken, and her voice was as gentle as ever.

"What they did to him left him in unimaginable pain. He would've never recovered. He would've suffered considerably for the rest of his life. He was unable to face that fate. It was something he had no control over. He knew you wouldn't suffer the same fate as him with Cindy and Phil having been caught."

"They guessed Cindy and her lover would turn up at the hospital to silence your father," Arthur took over, "so they set up a camera and recorded everything that was said and done. They have the evidence they need. They have Cindy's confession to murder and her intention to blame you. There's no escape for her this time. Your father doesn't want you to grieve for him. He's happy now. He's free from pain, and free from the shame of people knowing what was done to him. It'll all be in the newspapers once the case goes to court and sentences are passed. You will then be vindicated at last."

Lance couldn't understand why Blake needed to die. He could have taken something for the pain, and he had nothing to be ashamed of.

"Your father was ashamed of being tricked by the same young woman who had tricked him once before," Guinevere answered. "He was ashamed of being unable to have children of his own, and he was ashamed of forcing your parents into a relationship they originally hadn't wanted. He honestly believed everything would work out nicely, especially when your mother gave birth to you. He hadn't, however, taken human emotions into account, and he's not entirely to blame for that. It was simply the way he himself had been raised. He refused to let David play any part in your life. He refused to let David anywhere near you. Your mother only wanted to let him know how you were getting on in the beginning.

"David was interested in you. He had wanted to be involved, but he wasn't allowed the chance to do that. Blake convinced himself there was more going on between them, so he embarked on a series of affairs himself. That was the trigger that drove Nancy and David closer to each other. Then your mother realised that if she divorced Blake and married David, he could assume his rightful role as best he could without revealing his true identity. Blake at least agreed to that. None of them knew how David would react when seeing you after all those years. Blake's passing will make it a lot easier for you to get to know each other."

Lance was still convinced they could have worked something out. Blake didn't have to die. Arthur, however, told him that was his father's choice. It was far more complicated than just the issue of his true parentage. That could have easily been overcome. There were other issues as well. Lance obviously didn't realise the excruciating pain his father was in. He had wanted to pass over.

He could have easily stopped Cindy if he had really wanted to. It was the best solution for his father. Lance had gone to see him and had made peace with him. He was happy about that. Blake was proud of him, and he knew he thought no ill of him. He knew Lance didn't want to abandon him, despite the treatment he gave him. He was satisfied that Cindy would get nothing. It was time for him to pass over. He didn't want anything to spoil that moment. He didn't want to risk something else turning him against Lance.

He was looking on from a place of peace and tranquillity, knowing justice was finally done. He had found true happiness and contentment. He had found his own Avalon. He didn't want Lance to grieve for him. He wanted him to move on.

"I can't do that just yet," Lance said.

Gwyn gently rubbed his arm.

"Maybe you will in a few days' time. Your father is at peace, and that's what is important. He has won, in a way. He's beaten Cindy. His legacy is ensuring the world will now see her for the person she really is. He's succeeded in doing everything needed to ensure it will happen, thanks to your help. You don't need to do anything now. The truth will be revealed. Your father wants you to hold your head high and show the world how dignified you really are."

She paused a moment, and then she asked him if he was ready to go home. He should take a few days off work. She knew the others would understand. It would give him the chance to start picking up the pieces of his life. Lance hesitated then reluctantly stood up. Maybe he should consider what was best for his father. It was unfair to expect him to carry on while in unbearable pain. Maybe he should start looking to the future. Once this turmoil of emotions had subsided, it would be time for him to do just that.

Chapter Thirty-One

Gwyn left Cado in Lance's care and let herself outside. A blustery wind snatched leaves from the trees before swirling them around and carrying them away. There was a mixture of white and grey clouds scudding across the sky as they warned of the real possibility of rain. She wished for the briefest of moments as she hurried over to the office that she had pulled on her coat before venturing outside. She was opening the office door though, and she shuddered involuntarily as she closed it behind her again.

They had watched as the other three had arrived. The three were now taking off their coats as the computers started up. They looked round when Gwyn joined them. She reluctantly turned to face them and hesitated before speaking.

"Lance wants you all to know what happened in Boston, but he's not ready to talk about it himself yet. I've offered to come over and let you know."

The group listened, their eyes widening, as she explained.

"There won't be anything in the papers just yet," she finished, "not until after the court case. They're not being allowed to report on it until it's heard in court. Lance doesn't know how much influence the Petersons still have. He says he won't be surprised if Cindy gets away with it. His mum's doing everything she can to ensure justice is done. She's hired the best lawyers she can get hold of. She feels she owes it to Blake to make sure justice is served. She's arranging the funeral too, but we're not going to it though. Lance's mum fears we'll not be safe if we go over."

"Cindy Peterson has actually murdered Blake? How can that be possible?"

Anna's eyes were wide with shocked disbelief. Gwyn smiled sadly.

"Yes she's murdered Blake, and there was nothing Lance could do to stop her. He really did try his best. Phil was too strong for him, and the police didn't move quickly enough to stop her. Lance is really shaken up and upset at the moment. He was there, and he knew he could do nothing but watch Blake die. He's going to be rather irrational for a while. I can't see him concentrating on anything, so I don't see any point in him coming over here this week."

"Was Lance harmed in any way?" Rick asked. "With his behaviour when I brought him here last night, I'd feared they'd done something to him."

Gwyn shook her head.

"They didn't get the chance to do anything to him. We went to Avalon and spoke to Arthur and Guinevere. He's beginning to realise that what happened was best for Blake. We need to give him a few days to come to terms with what happened though. He does want to see you all really. He doesn't want to put off facing you. He just can't bring himself to explain what happened."

The group looked reluctant. They didn't know what to say. Rick eventually moved, and Will and Anna looked at each other before they followed him. Gwyn led the way back over to the house, where they found Lance in the kitchen. He was sitting on a chair by the table and had Cado perched on his lap. He looked up when the door opened and managed to hold their gaze for a few moments before he looked back at Cado again. His son was far too young to understand what had happened. He was oblivious to it all and played happily as though nothing had happened at all.

Gwyn filled the kettle and flicked it on before spooning coffee and sugar into five mugs. She warmed the milk formula in a bottle then handed it to Cado before making the coffee. Rick was already leading the commiserations after hearing what had happened. They wouldn't have wished it on Blake, despite everything he had said and done over the past year. He hadn't deserved what had been done to him.

"I can't change what's already happened," Lance spoke quietly. "I can't bring my father back. He said he didn't want me to dwell on my grief. He wants me to move on and start

165

to get to know my real father. I'm glad I went and made peace with him. He's proud of us all and everything we've achieved. And he was really glad you deceived him, Rick. The evidence is in the hands of a Boston newspaper now. They're going to reveal everything once the court case is over. King Arthur told me my father chose to die. He apologised to me for being a coward, and I think I'm beginning to understand what he means."

Blake didn't have the courage to face anyone after everything that was done to him. He instead chose the easy option when offered. He had left them to pick up the pieces and carry on without him. He had left them to endure the court case and live through all the sordid details to be raked up and put on public display for the world to see. He couldn't face the indignity of everyone knowing what a devious young woman had done to him. He had always been invincible. He couldn't be beaten. A weakness, however, had now been found and opened him up for ridicule. He couldn't live with the shame of being forced to endure that cruelty.

"Cindy and Phil are due to be charged today, so hopefully a date for the hearing will be set. I can't see that happening for months yet though. I have no choice but to go along with it. There's nothing I can do about it. I can't see Cindy pleading guilty. She's not that kind of person. I'm glad I'm here and well away from it all. I can only carry on as my father wanted," Lance hesitated, "which means there's something else you need to know."

Gwyn handed round the mugs of coffee and sat beside Lance. She made no attempt to take Cado from him. She knew he needed to hold onto his son at the moment. He really needed to hold something precious to him right now. Lance licked his lips.

"When my father realised what Cindy's really like, he made a new will in the presence of professionals who confirmed his sanity. He did everything he needed to do to prevent Cindy from being able to dispute it. I don't see it stopping her from trying, but I've been assured she'll get nowhere. My father has left everything to me. Mom brought a copy of the will with her when she last visited. It's the one thing my father was desperate for me to accept. When the funeral's over and everything's sorted out, I'll get everything. He doesn't want Cindy to get anything. I'm inheriting the company, and right now I honestly don't know that I really want it. I don't know what I'm going to do with it. I can't see us being able to incorporate it into our own company."

Lance looked across at the three after a long silence.

"What do I do with it?" he asked. "We already have enough to do here without having my father's company as well. I feel as though I owe it to my father to keep it though."

"There's no need for you to rush into anything," Rick told him, "just take your time. I don't want to see you doing anything rash. We'll think of something, if you want our help that is."

Lance gazed across at him and nodded. Everything felt surreal, as though he was standing on the outside and watching this happen to someone else. It was happening to him though. He was in the centre while everything revolved around him.

"Take a few days off," Rick said. "Get everything clear in your mind. We'll manage without you. You know where we are if you need to talk to us. I don't want to see you trying to work before next Monday. When the charges are brought and you have a better idea where you stand, we'll take things from there. I have a feeling King Arthur has everything under control though."

Lance sensed Gwyn smiling knowingly as he stared at Rick. He looked at her then back at Cado again. He knew everything was relatively easy for him. His mother and real father were directly involved with everything that was happening. They were living in Boston and facing the crowds asking countless questions that couldn't be answered just yet. They were arranging his father's funeral. Lance doubted that many people would go, and he couldn't risk travelling over again just yet. He really did have no choice this time. He was lucky last time. He had succeeded in fleeing from Boston before anyone recognised him with his longer hair and casual clothing. He couldn't take that chance again.

The day passed in a daze. Gwyn was settling Cado in his cot while Lance was in the living room when the phone began to ring. It was evening, and the lights glowed steadily. The curtains were pulled across the windows so they shut out the wind and rain. He stared at the ringing phone before he eventually and reluctantly answered it.

He was surprised to hear Nancy's voice. He was still talking to her when Gwyn joined him. He looked as though he was unable to believe what his mother was telling him. Gwyn said nothing as she patiently waited for the conversation to end. Lance stared into space when he slowly lowered the phone and placed it back onto its cradle. He couldn't take in what he had just been told. He eventually looked at Gwyn.

"Mom went to court to hear the charges being brought against Cindy and Phil," he said. "She said they've both pleaded guilty. They're not disputing anything. I can't believe it's as good as over."

Gwyn hugged him and smiled. His arms immediately surrounded her so he could hold her tightly. She could guess what this meant to him. Cindy no doubt believed her actions would pass unnoticed by avoiding a very public court hearing. She couldn't have known that the papers were now free to publish everything they knew. She was about to get the publicity she believed she had avoided. Nancy would undoubtedly be ecstatic. Lance was obviously relieved to have at least been spared one ordeal. They only needed to get the funeral out of the way. They would maybe then be able to draw a line beneath this whole sorry saga and move on.

Chapter Thirty-Two

Gwyn watched Lance walk across to the office from the kitchen window. She couldn't pretend that the past few days had been easy. Lance's mind had been in a complete turmoil as he desperately tried to think of what he could have done differently so he could save his father's life. He had reached the same conclusion every time though. Phil Jameson was too strong for him, and King Arthur had done nothing to help him. He could never release himself from Phil's grip without Arthur's help. Arthur had chosen to help Blake achieve his ultimate goal instead. Lance still didn't want to contemplate what would have happened to him if the police hadn't turned up and stopped Cindy and Phil when they did.

Gwyn had taken him to Avalon every day. He had needed telling over and over that the outcome really was best for his father. It had almost been as though Blake had planned it from the very start. Lance still felt cheated. He had always looked upon his father as the one person who could resolve anything. He had been unbeatable. He had been a real titan among men. And yet, in the end, he had just given up and accepted his fate. He had acted completely out of character. Lance had expected him to fight to the bitter end. He had expected him to ensure the Petersons, and Cindy in particular, were brought crashing down.

Rick had arrived when Lance had decided to cross to the office. Rick knew Lance well enough to know when something was wrong, and Gwyn knew he would keep an eye on her young husband. The three at least knew what had happened. All explanations were given, and Blake's funeral was due to be held in a couple of days. They didn't know how many people would attend, but they only expected Nancy and David to be there.

Gwyn and Lance hadn't watched any news programmes. They didn't want to watch, and they didn't have to watch.

Nancy had kept them well-informed about what was happening. The media circus had well and truly begun following Cindy's admission of guilt. They had, by all accounts, revealed every last gruesome and gory detail to an ever-hungry public. Any thoughts of a cover up on Cindy's part had quickly faded and dissolved away. Everything that Cindy Peterson had planned to do—and actually done—to Lance and Blake was now common knowledge. It was still the only topic of conversation in Boston.

Gwyn watched Lance disappear into the office and waited until the door was closed before she turned away from the window. Nancy was, from what Gwyn could gather, revelling in the media attention. She was already quick to blame the people of Boston for driving her son away with the way they had treated him like a pariah. Lance had done nothing wrong, and yet he had been treated as though he was the villain. He needed time to come to terms with everything that had happened. He needed privacy in which to think about everything he had witnessed.

Gwyn picked Cado up out of his high chair and carried him through to the living room. She played with him for a while, and occasionally looked at the picture of Lance stitched with the chart her mother had designed. She too had initially questioned why Arthur hadn't stepped in to help prevent Blake's murder. She had slowly begun to understand why. Blake had been right to fear something else turning him against Lance. He would also have been ridiculed relentlessly, a ridicule that ultimately would have incited him to take action to damage countless people. Lance would have been the first to suffer. Arthur's only concern was to protect his young prodigy.

Gwyn checked the time. She changed Cado's nappy, pulled on his coat and strapped him into his pushchair. She had only ventured out to Avalon with Lance over the last few days. She knew she needed to restock the larder soon, a task she wasn't sure Lance was ready to face yet.

She pulled on her coat, pushed her purse into her pocket and stepped outside. She crossed to the office, let herself inside and closed the door once she and Cado were safely in the room. Lance was talking business with Rick and Will, and they all looked round when Gwyn joined them. They were deliberately avoiding the subject that was Blake Brookes. The other three, in reality, needed Lance to mention him first before they discussed him. They all knew it was something they couldn't avoid forever.

Anna was glad to escape from the office. She didn't know what to say or do now Lance was back. They were all wary and nervously wondering how they should act. It inevitably brought a certain tension to the office, though Lance in fairness was doing his best to behave as normally as possible. It wasn't easy for any of them.

"I'm really sorry, but I have no idea what I should say," Anna blurted out. "I can't imagine what it must be like for you."

She was walking down the drive towards the lane beside Gwyn.

"It's slowly getting easier. Lance needs time to let it sink in properly. A lot's happened lately. We haven't seen any news programmes. We've refused to watch them."

"They've gone into an awful lot of detail," Anna informed. "Too much detail really. I'm surprised by the way Lance is trying so hard to act normally."

"We're lucky. We can go to Avalon to visit Arthur and Guinevere. It's really helped him come to terms with what's happened. Arthur and Guinevere have contacted his father and told him what he said. They've explained why his father decided to pass over. It's helped bring some sense to it all and make it easier to deal with. He was in an awful lot of pain, and he would have always been in pain for the rest of his life. He'd have had no control over it, and he couldn't face that. That's what confused Lance the most. His father was always a fighter, so it was totally out of character."

Gwyn paused a moment before deciding to continue.

"He was ashamed as well. He was ashamed of being unable to have children of his own. He was convinced everyone would think less of him because of that. He was also ashamed of having been so easily made a fool of, not once but twice, by the same person. He knew he'd never have the same social standing again. He died happy though. Lance was with him to the very end, and he still looked upon him as his father despite being told otherwise. He was the one who raised him, in a fashion. He was the one Lance always looked up to and begrudgingly admired. Lance, in the end, proved what he was capable of achieving when given the chance. His father is very proud of him and pleased he's still looked upon as his father. Once he's laid to rest, Lance will be able to get to know his real father. There will be nothing and no one to get in the way and confuse him."

Gwyn slowed suddenly and stared at the sold board standing against the fence of a cottage. She then looked at Anna.

"It's nothing to do with us," Anna said. "We're buying a house on the outskirts of Bristol. Guinevere was right about the manor house I was admiring. It looks really impressive from here, but when we viewed it we saw exactly how much needs doing to it. It really would've been a nightmare. I'm so glad I heeded Guinevere's warning. The house we are buying is plenty big enough for us, and it needs hardly anything doing to it."

Gwyn smiled knowingly. She was glad that Anna had chosen to listen to Guinevere.

"You know we're going to get lost in our new house," Anna continued. "We've been in our terraced house with its little concrete back yard for so long. We're hoping it'll sell quickly, with it being in a popular area. We'll be moving from that two bedroomed terrace to a big five bedroomed detached house with a large garden."

"You've both worked hard," Gwyn said, "and you've dared to believe. It's your reward."

They had reached the centre of the village and the store they were heading to. Gwyn left Anna to post off her packages and gathered the groceries she needed. She moved to the till and answered all the questions asked about Lance.

"I've started to have the press come in," Mary warned. "They're asking questions and getting ready to pounce. They're hungry for answers. I can't see them respecting your wish for privacy for much longer."

Gwyn looked worried as she thanked the shopkeeper. She knew they couldn't avoid the subject any longer. Lance needed to meet the press and give them the answers they were seeking. She wasn't sure he was ready for that yet, and she knew there was only one way of finding out.

She and Anna quickly walked back to the house. The trees lining the drive sheltered them from the worst of the wind. It all looked so tranquil and serene with the hills rising up behind the house. Gwyn looked at the scene before her. She wasn't looking forward to being invaded by an army of journalists. She reluctantly admitted to preferring them all coming at the same time to have them visit one by one.

She hesitated for the briefest of moments then followed Anna into the office.

"We need to talk," she announced. "Mary's just told me the press are ready to pounce with a multitude of questions. I think it'd be better to meet them all in one go to answer those questions. They'll hopefully leave us alone then Lance."

He was silent as he gazed at her. He was initially gripped with panic, a panic from which he was already beginning to recover from. Maybe he should face them all. They weren't going to go away until he had.

"Let's break for a coffee so I can work out how best to deal with this," he said.

Gwyn nodded and headed over to the house. Cado had, at least, fallen asleep. She left him in his pushchair, switched on the kettle and made the coffee as the others joined her. They didn't know where to begin as they sat around the kitchen table. How did they contact the media to arrange the mass meeting Gwyn had suggested?

"I don't want them coming here," Lance said.

"Why not use the conference room at your father's offices in Bristol?" Rick suggested. "You have inherited his company after all. You're entitled to use the building, and it'll stop the press intruding into your personal space here. Will and I could go with you if you want."

Lance gazed at him and eventually began to nod slowly. It was the simplest way of keeping them away from Gwyn and Cado. He needed to talk things through and get everything straight in his mind first though. He needed to phone his mother too and talk to her. He was suddenly being forced to face up to everything that had happened. He had to accept it and actually talk about it to complete strangers. It made it very real, and right now, he just wanted it all to be over with.

Chapter Thirty-Three

Gwyn put the phone back and looked back round at Cado. He was contentedly playing with his toys while oblivious to anything else going on around him. He was such a happy child—a child who rarely cried. Gwyn smiled as she crossed to where he was sitting on the floor. How different it must have been for Lance when he had grown up. He was determined to ensure his own son didn't suffer in the way he had. Cado's life was destined to be so different to his fathers'.

She picked Cado up and carried him to the office. She closed the door then put him back down. She looked at Anna and guessed she had heard from Will when she had heard from Lance just now. The press conference was over, and the three men had decided to stay and meet the staff at the office. She understood they planned to be back here before the afternoon was over.

Everything seemed to have happened so quickly. The three men had travelled to the Bristol offices as soon as Lance had decided to meet the press so they could see the people still working there. Rick had needed a few days to arrange the conference, but it was now all over. Lance had faced the media circus and answered all their questions. There were still issues that needed discussing.

The funeral had been held, and Nancy and David were now planning to visit them. They had a lot that they needed to talk about. Lance had spoken to both of them on the phone, but they all knew it wasn't the same as meeting face to face. That was what they really needed to do.

Gwyn invited Anna over for a coffee and led the way back to the house. She sat Cado in his high chair with a bottle of milk and some pieces of carrot and apple to keep him occupied as she made the coffee. She handed a mug to Anna and joined her at the table.

"How are you getting on with your houses?" she asked.

"The new house should be ours by the end of this week. I want to move in straight away, but Will wants to get the work done before we do that. He's right of course. He's always been sensible. I just want to be there and living the dream. We've had a couple of viewings on our terraced house, but I think our things are cluttering the house and putting people off. Will's sure it'll sell soon."

Anna sighed with frustration.

"To be honest, I think Will's preoccupied with the system ordered by the Mercer chain. I know I can't really complain about it though. We've been completely inundated with enquiries since the deal struck with the Cosmopolitan Hotel chain. It takes time, and I'm well aware of companies not being prepared to wait for too long."

Gwyn hummed.

"It sounds as though you could do with some help. Do you think the Brookes company might be able to provide it? Lance does own that too now after all."

"I don't know. I don't know if Will would be able to trust them with the task. I can suggest it though. It must be worth discussing." Anna hesitated. "How is Lance really feeling now?"

"He still has his ups and downs. His parents are going to fly over to visit soon now the funeral's over. I'm sure he'll be glad to get this first meeting over with. He was in no fit state to acknowledge his real father when he was in Boston. This'll be their first proper meeting since he was told the truth. It's bound to be awkward at first, but I'm sure everything will be alright. They just need some time together to sort out how they really feel. They've got on really well in the past, so I see no reason why they shouldn't do so again."

They weren't denying that they had an awful lot of catching up to do. Gwyn was under no delusion of how awkward and tense the atmosphere would be when Lance's parents arrived. They had to have this first meeting at some time, and it would be best to have it sooner to get it over with so it didn't constantly prey on their minds. Lance had been through a roller coaster of emotions since discovering the truth. No one was denying that the last couple of years had been one life-changing experience after another. Gwyn smiled. Lance's wasn't the only life that had been changed. His coming had affected them all.

Gwyn was glad to see Rick's car heading along the drive to the yard. Rick and Will headed to the office while Lance walked towards the house instead. He looked tired but relieved, and he was clearly glad it was over at last. He had had Rick and Will on either side of him with their support. One of them had spoken for him when he couldn't answer a question. He had confirmed how difficult his time with Cindy Peterson had been, particularly during his last year with her. He had fortunately had Rick's full support though. He wouldn't have got through it without his help and the woman who had since become his wife.

Lance found Gwyn waiting in the kitchen when he let himself into the house. She was making some coffee. He looked across at her then wrapped his arms around her and held her closely against him. The worst was now over. He had dared to venture out in public again. He had faced the press, answered all their questions as best he could and then met the staff still employed in his father's offices. They had told him how glad they were to learn he was now in charge. They had told him how awful the working conditions were when Blake, and especially Cindy, had been there.

Gwyn led Lance through to the living room and sat him on the settee so they could watch Cado playing with his toys. Lance gazed at his son as though totally transfixed. His own childhood had been so different. He wasn't allowed any toys. He had instead been expected to only show an interest in computers. He had now discovered the tyrant hadn't been his father at all. He had gone over his life so far over the last few days and tried to analyse every last detail he thought of.

"Do you think he'd have treated me any differently if he had been my real father?" he asked suddenly.

He eventually tore his eyes away from Cado and looked at Gwyn when getting no answer.

"I don't know," she said. "I have a feeling we'll never know. If he had fathered a son, he wouldn't have been you. You're who you are because David is your real father. I don't suppose Blake would've treated his own son differently. I suspect he'd have treated him in the same way he himself was treated. It's how you'd have reacted by being a different person that we'll never know."

Lance stared at the coffee table and said nothing. He believed that, if he had been a lot more like Blake Brookes, then he'd have in all probability stood up to him. There would undoubtedly have been a real clash of temperaments and no end of conflicts. He wouldn't have been awestruck when first clasping eyes on Avalon. He wouldn't have wanted to find out more. He wouldn't have been attracted to Gwyn. He wouldn't be living here now…

Lance sighed with frustration. He was angry with them all—with his parents and Blake. He was angry with the way they had deceived him. He was, however, also thankful with the way his life had turned out. He claimed he had forgiven them all, but he knew that claim wasn't actually true. He would never know if he would have come here if his mother had left Blake for David and taken him with her years ago. His whole life could have been so different. He could have met and married someone else. He might have never been involved with Cindy Peterson. He might have never discovered Avalon…

He had found it strange being back in his father's offices again today. It had all looked so familiar. He didn't know if he could reorganise it all, especially as they were busy with the Mercer contract Will was currently working on. Gwyn smiled in her usual quiet way.

"Does it really need to be reorganised that much? Maybe you could do the same as I did with the shop in Glastonbury. Perhaps you could involve the staff, ask for their suggestions for any possible changes. You don't have to implement them all. I appreciate you have a lot of work on at the moment. I don't need Anna to tell me that. Could you consider getting the staff at your father's company to help you with it? You wouldn't need to go over there that often if you put someone you really trust in charge of the day to day running. You'd be able to concentrate much more on your work here. It doesn't have to be that big a problem. You'd only really need the right person in charge."

Lance glanced at her then suddenly relaxed and smiled. He was too young and inexperienced to be given this responsibility. He wanted to enjoy his time with his wife and children. He didn't want to be burdened down by his father's company. He was worried, however, about making the wrong choice. He didn't want to let his father down. He needed a constant reassurance that he was doing the right thing. He didn't want to prove to be the massive disappointment and failure that Cindy accused him of being. Their small company was nothing like the one they had left behind.

Lance knew that Gwyn was his biggest ally. She had a talent for looking at things differently and made everything so much simpler. He in contrast made everything far more complicated than they needed to be. In her own quiet way, Gwyn actually coped far better than he could. She looked after Cado. She kept the house clean and tidy. She created new tapestry designs. She ran her shop in Glastonbury. And on top of all of that, she was carrying his second child while also giving him the support he needed. She looked for nothing in return. Without her, he really would be nothing.

"I don't know what I'd do without you," he said. "You make everything so easy."

"I've never believed in making things complicated. That only makes it easier to make mistakes. You're not like your... Blake, and you'd have never been like him. It's just not in your nature to be like him. The company is yours now. You don't have to run it in the way your father did. It's yours to run in the way that suits you. It'll only dominate your life if you let it. Don't let it dictate what you do. Show it that you're the one in charge. I'm sure there must be people you can trust to run it for you on a daily basis. You'd only need to go in to deal with the issues only you can then. People like you and they'll want to help you. You only need to believe in it for it to reward you. You can prove to everyone that you're more than capable. You can prove the critics wrong. Don't forget who's supporting us. You can't possibly fail."

Lance smiled as a quiet confidence grew inside him. He had the support of King Arthur. He was King Arthur. He couldn't possibly fail.

Chapter Thirty-Four

Gwyn heard a car stop in the yard. She looked out the kitchen window then switched on the kettle. The three men had been gone all day. They had at last returned now the afternoon was almost over. Lance climbed out of the car and hesitated before turning towards the house. There was no point in starting any more work today, even if he did have the energy and enthusiasm to do so. He was glad to get back home so he could join Gwyn again. The others were, after all, perfectly capable of locking the office.

He let himself into the kitchen and looked at Gwyn while putting a large pile of paperwork on the table. Today had stretched on for an eternity. He had needed to go to the Bristol offices though. He had needed to have the dreaded meeting with the staff. The company was in complete disarray, with no one seeming to know what they were doing. He needed to go back at least once more before everything was sorted. He had felt so positive and optimistic when they had gone in this morning. He now felt totally drained and exhausted. It was a complete nightmare. It was by far the worst thing he had needed to deal with.

Cado wasn't interested in Lance's day as he sat in his high chair and played with his toys. Gwyn put two mugs of coffee onto the table. She made Lance sit down then stood behind him and began to massage his shoulders.

"Why don't you tackle one problem at a time? Let's eat, then maybe you'll tell me what happened."

Lance barely glanced at her as he suddenly relaxed a little. He already knew she would make everything so simple. Will had spent most of the day changing the company's security system. The Petersons, with Cindy in custody and her parents under investigation, weren't an immediate threat. That could change all too easily, and there had to be others who could, and would, take advantage of the current weak security of the company. Will's priority had rightly been to safeguard what Lance did have. Lance and Rick had been left to meet the staff. They had talked for hour after hour. They had listened to all the grievances and made notes. They were left with having to discuss which changes to implement.

Lance was in no doubt of the extent Cindy had succeeded to demoralise the staff. He was giving them the chance to make suggestions and the changes needed to improve their working environment. He and Rick had let them speak. They had patiently listened to them before then asking what changes they would like to make. It was now partly down to the staff. They would only have themselves to blame if they were still unhappy. They had appeared a little happier when the three men left. Lance still had a long list of grievances to look through before he next went to Bristol though. He sighed with frustration as he felt defeated.

"I know it's definitely going to be at least ten times worse in Boston," he said. "I don't really want to go over there. I know I can't ignore it though. I know it's not going to go away. I know I'm going to have to face them some time, and I know it'll be far worse if I put it off for too long."

"Your mum and dad are flying over tomorrow. Maybe they'll be able to help you out."

"Mom's got her shop to run."

Lance spoke far too quickly. He then looked round at her. His mother did have her shop to run. Neither of them was denying that. His father worked for a different company though, and he knew everything he needed to know about computers. He was the original brains behind Blake's empire, and he lived in Boston. He couldn't trust anyone else more. David had helped them set up their company, and he was due to arrive here tomorrow.

"Do you think my father will help me?" he asked.

"You could ask. At worst he'll say no, and that needn't be the end of the world."

Lance gazed into space as his mind drifted slightly.

"Arthur and Guinevere knew who he really was when they first met him didn't they. It's obvious now I look back. Their expressions showed they knew his secret. I guess keeping that secret was the right thing to do back then. The time wasn't right for me to know. I'd have never believed them, and I doubt I'd have accepted David into my life."

A few short months had made such a difference. Blake had disowned him at Christmas, and he had left him nothing. That had, in a way, been a huge relief. He hadn't wanted to inherit the company. He had now discovered Blake wasn't his real father at all. Blake was now dead, and he had ensured everything he owned was left to him before he passed over. Everything he loathed greatly was now his. Blake had desperately wanted him to accept it all. How could he possibly refuse?

Lance watched Gwyn load the dishwasher. He then stood up, picked Cado up and led the way to the living room. The grass in the garden had grown well. It was now well on the way to establishing a thick lawn. The shrubs that had been planted were beginning to fill out. It would all look so much better next summer. Cado would also be a year older with a younger brother or sister. Maybe he would have tamed Blake's company by then so he could possibly even begin to enjoy it all.

The company was the last thing he wanted to think about right now. He wanted to think about Gwyn and Cado. He wanted everything else to be forced to wait until tomorrow. Gwyn's words echoed in his mind—*don't let it dominate your life like it did your father's.* If nothing else, that was the one thing he was determined to do.

Gwyn opened the window to air the room and made up the bed in the guest bedroom. She knew that, with Lance having just left for the airport, he would be some time before he returned with his parents. There was nothing else she could do with the bed made before they arrived. Cado played quietly. He was unaware of the imminent arrival of their visitors. There would be no secret to uncover for him. David would have always been Lance's father. There would be no confusion and no mixed emotions over the lies that had been lived.

The door opened at last, and Lance and his parents joined them in the living room. Coffee was made while cases were taken to the bedroom. There was some inevitable tension in the air. This was, after all, the first proper meeting between Lance and David since the truth was revealed. They felt awkward and unsure of how the other would react. They needed time to adjust to the revelation. None of them pretended it was going to be easy.

"The funeral was quiet," Nancy broke the silence. "A few local businessmen turned up. They looked really uncomfortable and didn't know what to say. Most people were too embarrassed to attend. They've heard the truth, and a lot of them have realised how wrong they were to support the Petersons. They're starting to withdraw their support and turn their backs on them."

Lance said nothing. There was nothing that he wanted to say. He wasn't interested in how the people of Boston were reacting.

"Loads of people came to the shop to see me," Nancy continued. "They're really sorry about how they've treated you, Lance. They know Blake's left everything to you. They want to know when you're going to the offices in Boston."

Lance looked down at the carpet.

"I don't know yet. I haven't decided. I know I have to go over some time, and sooner rather than later. I don't know that I can face everyone just yet. I know it'll get harder the longer I leave it."

Lance licked his lips and dared to look at David.

"Actually, I was wondering if you'd help me out. We were over at the Bristol offices yesterday, and it's in a mess. I hate to think what the Boston offices are like. I know I have to go over and find out how bad it is. I don't want to go on my own though. Rick's offered to go with me, but I had a chat with him and Will earlier this morning. I want to put someone I trust in charge of running the Boston offices so I don't have to keep going over there. I'm hoping you'll agree to do that for me. I can't think of anyone else I can trust or who's better qualified."

Lance's nerves gripped him as David stared at him. He felt a need to talk on.

"You effectively set up the empire, so you more than anyone knows the basis the company is built up from. You've also helped us here, so I know you're more than capable of doing the job. I know I'll have to fly over to Boston, but if you agree to take on the job, it'll mean Rick won't need to go with me."

Lance suddenly stopped talking. He was being unfair. He should be giving David time to consider the offer being made. He shouldn't expect an immediate answer. David looked stunned as he stared into space. Nancy, for once, was actually lost for words. They were taken completely by surprise by the offer made. David found his voice after a long and tense silence.

"I won't be able to start straight away. I'll need to hand in my resignation."

He hadn't expected or anticipated the offer being made. He had been taken by surprise. Accepting the offer wasn't an issue. He was going to need time to get used to the idea of returning to where he had started out all those years ago. It felt unreal and surreal. They had expected this visit to be tense and nerve-racking. They had expected to feel awkward in each other's company. They were instead distracted by Lance's offer and starting to make plans for the future. Life was about to change for them all once again.

Chapter Thirty-Five

Gwyn was used to falling asleep while lying in Lance's arms. Last night though she had slept alone. She hadn't had his comforting arms around her making her feel safe and secure. She hated being parted from him, but she knew why he needed to fly over to Boston. Nancy and David were with him, and someone who was very important to them had gone too. King Arthur was by his side and ready as always to protect him in an instant.

The last few days had passed in a complete whirl. They hadn't expected David to accept Lance's offer so readily. It had caught Lance off-guard, and it had left them with a monumental list of things to discuss. They had talked for hours as they worked their way through every item until every detail was finally decided. Lance was left with no obstacle in his way to prevent him from travelling to Boston.

The original reason for Nancy and David's visit had somehow been forgotten amid all the discussions. The tension and nervousness had dissolved away by the time they were ready to board an aeroplane at Bristol airport. Lance had flown to America with his parents as though they had done nothing else for his whole life. The only thing to spoil the trip was the fact he had left Gwyn and Cado behind.

Rick had watched the aeroplane take off before he returned to the office. Gwyn had watched his car turn onto the road before she cleaned the guest bedroom and bathroom. She hated being separated from Lance, but she hadn't really wanted to go to Boston. Arthur and Guinevere had assured her the atmosphere really had changed for the better. She was still wary of the reception he would receive though. She hadn't argued with him when he insisted she and Cado stayed here. He hadn't wanted her to fly, especially as this was, purely and simply, a business trip. He wanted them to stay here while he and David started to sort out the Boston offices and he decided what to do with Blake's apartment and country house.

Gwyn settled Cado into his pushchair and emerged from the house. She needed to continue their normal routine for his sake. Anna was ready to walk to the village. She stood up as soon as Gwyn opened the office door. They left Rick and Will to their work and headed along the lane. The traffic was quieter now the summer rush was over. Their walk wasn't as traumatic now as it had been over the past two months. They could relax a little more, and Anna was eager to tell Gwyn about their new house as they returned from the store. The house was almost ready for them to move in to, and with a buyer for their terraced house, the move couldn't come quickly enough.

Gwyn smiled quietly. Everything had happened so quickly. She hadn't known any of these people three years ago. She had known hardly anyone. She had been happy and contented with the life she had been living. She now knew so many people. She was married to Lance. She had given him a son, and she was expecting his second child. She hadn't expected to witness anyone breaking the spell cast by Morgan, as so many had failed over the centuries. Lance, however, had succeeded. He had broken the spell imprisoning Arthur on Avalon. Avalon itself had then been threatened. They had managed to protect it and safeguard its very existence so it could, and had, return to them. They had a beautiful home, her shop in Glastonbury and the increasingly successful business built up by the three men from nothing.

The past year hadn't been easy. Lance had been in complete turmoil since discovering Blake wasn't his biological father. She had supported him as best she could as he rode a rollercoaster of emotions. He was beginning to come to terms with it all at last, except for one thing. His initial disappointment in Blake just accepting his fate had slowly turned to anger, an anger that threatened to consume him. After a lifetime of begrudgingly admiring this man, he felt increasingly badly let down by him. He hadn't once looked upon him as a coward.

Blake's past actions had finally caught up with him. He was exposed as a bully and cheating womaniser with no regard for anyone but himself. He was the powerful one, the lord of a mighty empire who couldn't be toppled. He knew in the end he only had himself to blame for his own downfall. He was too proud, and he was all too easily flattered by Cindy's charm. He had blindly walked into her trap, and he had paid the ultimate price for her betrayal.

Gwyn snapped out of her trance when she heard Anna speak. She blushed with embarrassment and apologised for not listening to her. She didn't mean to be rude, but she needed to see Guinevere. They were close to the driveway and were soon able to step off the lane. She left Anna to make her way to the office and disappeared among the trees. Cado was sleeping quietly as she pushed him to the shores of the lake. Guinevere was just stepping off the boat when they emerged from the trees. Gwyn stopped the pushchair while still at a safe distance from the shoreline and greeted the queen.

"I'm a little confused," she confessed.

She was seeking answers to the questions in her mind. She didn't need to ask them out loud for the queen to hear her. Guinevere smiled kindly.

"Lance is perfectly safe. There's no hostility towards him in Boston now. We'd have never let him go if there had been the slightest hint of danger. He has a lot to do over there, which will keep his mind occupied. Blake and Cindy stirred up a lot of ill-will among the workforce in the Boston offices. Like the people in Bristol, they've lost their way. They all need guidance to get them back on the right track. David is well known over there, and he'll be remembered by some of the staff. He's the best person to lead them forwards. That he's Lance's true father will be an advantage. They'll get the problems sorted out in a few days. Lance will then be able to return home."

Gwyn was silent as she took in Guinevere's words. She then looked back at the queen again.

"There's something else I need to know. If none of this had happened, if Blake hadn't been fooled by Cindy, would Lance have ever discovered his true identity?"

Guinevere pondered over the question for a moment or two.

"I believe the truth would have eventually been revealed yes. The opportune moment would have arisen. It would've given Lance's mother and two fathers the chance to confess all to him. It wouldn't have turned into such a public spectacle with its spectacular outcome though. They would've worked through everything together and reached an amicable agreement. In reality, that's the only thing that Lance has been robbed of."

Gwyn gazed into space. Lance had felt cheated out of the opportunity to make peace with the man he believed was his father for most of his life. He blamed Cindy for snatching that opportunity away from him. He also felt angry at Blake for not fighting. The more he thought about it all, the angrier he became. He now found it almost impossible to forgive Blake for giving up so easily. He felt abandoned and left to work through this alone. He really needed a meeting with Blake before he could begin to move on.

Guinevere doubted that Blake Brookes would agree to such a meeting. He feared rejection, and so preferred to avoid facing Lance again. He knew he had been exposed as a bully and a coward. He was now unwilling to admit to anyone that the accusations were right. She couldn't see Blake agreeing to meet Lance one last time. He anticipated questions he would find awkward to answer. She could make no promises. She could only do her best to convince Blake to meet Lance.

Gwyn nodded and watched Guinevere step back onto her boat. The boat then drifted away as though being propelled by an unseen underwater force. Gwyn kept her eyes upon the boat and its solitary occupant until it disappeared into the mist that surrounded the island. The scene was so tranquil and calm it encouraged her to stay for a while. She knew Cado would soon wake up and would want something to eat though.

She made her way back out of the trees and headed into the house. She warmed a bottle of milk as Cado began to stir. She smiled at him then looked round when she heard a knock on the door. It opened slightly, and she relaxed as Rick stepped inside.

"I'm sure Lance will be fine," he said.

Gwyn picked Cado up and sat him in his high chair.

"Of course he will," she agreed, "especially as King Arthur's gone with him."

"So what's the problem?"

Gwyn gave Cado the bottle of milk and looked back at Rick.

"Lance is having trouble coming to terms with losing his… Blake. He was disappointed with how he just gave up. He's now getting angrier that he didn't fight Cindy to the bitter end. It wasn't what he expected from the man who had always appeared invincible. He's started to ask questions, and he's looking for answers he feels he can't get. I went to see Guinevere to see if she can get some of those answers by the time he comes home. I fear it's stopping him from being able to move on and get to know his real father. What he really needs is to meet Blake so he can directly ask him the questions he has. If Blake refuses then I believe he really will have been cheated."

It was all down to Guinevere and her powers of persuasion. Time was against her though. There was no denying she had a lot to do.

Chapter Thirty-Six

Lance was away for almost two weeks. He phoned Gwyn every day he was away, until he at last told her he was on his way home. The time dragged as Gwyn watched expectantly from a window for Rick's car. Her excitement at every car on the road quickly turned to disappointment as each one continued on to its unknown destination. One car eventually turned onto the driveway. Gwyn's heart leapt up her throat as she picked up Cado and hurried outside.

Lance looked relaxed and content as he climbed out of the car. He greeted them, took Cado from Gwyn and carried him back into the house. He was as glad to be back at home as Gwyn was. She reluctantly let him go so she could give Cado a bottle of milk and make them some coffee. Cado was wide awake and not even remotely ready to relinquish his hold on his father. He was allowed to stay up later than usual, and he still objected strongly when taken to his cot. He wanted his father to stay with him. Lance remained calm and insistent when he eventually left Cado to settle for the night.

He pulled the bedroom door shut and turned his attention to his wife. He had noticed her patience as she let Cado successfully vie for his undivided attention. It was her turn now. She had tidied away Cado's toys and made some coffee while he had settled their son in his room. He wasn't interested in sitting here and talking though. He'd been parted from her for two weeks and only had one thing on his mind. Cado's refusal to leave him had been more than a little frustrating.

Gwyn willingly followed when he led her upstairs. She had ached for him from the moment she knew he was returning home. She was at last lying in his arms and nestling comfortably against him as she gently caressed his skin with her fingers. He was here with her again. She could feel him against her and the sensation was very real. He was calm and relaxed, the change in him surprising after the tension and upheaval of the last few months. They weren't seeking an explanation just yet. Their overwhelming lust for each other was satisfied and they were taking a few minutes to recover as they refused to let go of each other.

"How did you get on in Boston?" Gwyn asked eventually.

"OK I guess," he answered. "Actually we've done better than OK. Some of the staff remembered my father from years ago. It helped get them on side when we told them he'll be in overall charge of running those offices when he's finished working his resignation. They weren't anything like as hostile when I left. I think we've sorted the problems we were facing."

"What about everyone else in Boston? How're they treating you?"

"They seem to have come round. It was really awkward and difficult at first. Their behaviour was well over the top when I first arrived. It was embarrassing really, especially when mom was about. She kept reminding them how they behaved before. I had to plead with her to say no more in the end. She'd made her point and really needed to drop the subject before she turned everyone against her."

"And your real father, how're you getting on with him now?"

Lance hesitated as she patiently waited for an answer.

"We're getting on OK. We've been really busy, with him going to work before we tried to sort out the problems at my… Blake's company. We've not had chance to talk about our relationship. We've been too tired in the evenings to discuss anything. Besides, the evenings were when mom told us how her shop's doing. I know we need to discuss it at some time, but everything's just too manic at the moment for us to do that just yet. I'm sure we'll be able to make time once everything has settled down again."

Lance rolled onto his side so he faced her. He didn't want to discuss any of that right now. Right now was about just the two of them and no one else. She smiled at him and didn't resist him as any thoughts of anyone else disappeared from her mind. This moment was about just the two of them. No one else mattered. They were totally wrapped up in each other and giving no thought to anyone else. They could do that tomorrow, when Cado was awake and the other three were in the office. They wanted to make the most of this time they had before others inevitably joined them.

Rick, Will and Anna were surprised when the office door opened and Lance stepped into the room. He held Cado as the toddler again refused to let him go. They hadn't expected to see Lance today. They had expected him to remain indoors with Gwyn and Cado. He wanted to see them though. He wanted to tell them how he had got on in America. The atmosphere in Boston really had changed for the better for him. The hostility was gone and replaced with a sense of embarrassment and a deep regret for their recent behaviour towards him.

The Petersons were the ones now being hounded out of town. They had been exposed, with even some of those most loyal to them turning their backs on them in disgust. Their sales had taken a massive nosedive, while the number of enquiries made to Blake's company steadily increased. He wasn't the social outcast now. That title belonged to the Petersons. Blake hadn't deserved what they had done to him, despite being admired but disliked.

Lance was now accepted as the new owner of Blake's company. He wasn't known in Boston, despite his previous time there, as well as he was in Bristol. All the staff had understandably been wary of him at first. David's presence and imminent involvement, however, had helped enormously. He was known and well-respected in Boston. That he was Lance's true father wasn't yet being openly discussed in Lance's presence. He had sensed that everyone had known, and he had sensed they were either too embarrassed or too unsure of him to mention it just yet. Lance was sure that, in time, they would talk about it, and maybe even accept it as though it had always been.

"What's the next step?" Rick asked.

"I need to go over to the Bristol offices again soon. Not today though. I noticed a lot of untapped talent in the Boston offices. I suspect there will be some in Bristol too. I'd like us all to visit the Boston offices when everything's settled down. I think we can work with the staff in both offices. What do you say about the possibility of amalgamating their hardware with our software? We might be able to even develop further in the future. We do seem to be getting bogged down at the moment. I think you've become the victim of your own success Will."

Lance hesitated, as though waiting for some kind of response. No one said anything though, so he dared to continue.

"I'm wondering if it'd be best if we ask some of the Bristol people to have a go at developing a couple of the systems requested. It'd free you up to check their work when completed and make any necessary adjustments before signing them off and delivering them. We'd get through more work and we'll not need to turn any potential customers away."

Will gazed at him and seemed to give in. He could see what Lance was suggesting. He had to admit that, if he was brutally honest, he was struggling with the workload. Maybe there was no shame in asking for help.

Lance invited the trio for a coffee. Will only needed help because he was so successful. He was finally admitting that he needed help to fulfil the orders they had. He needed to start trusting others. He couldn't do it all by himself. There was far too much that needed doing. It was turning into a nightmare that was running his entire life. He needed to take charge.

Gwyn handed a bottle of milk to Cado and then handed round mugs of coffee. The toddler was still refusing to let go of his father, as though fearful of being deserted again. Gwyn sat down beside Lance. She knew better than to try and take Cado away from him. He would settle again in time and give Lance the time and space he needed to get back to work. Today wasn't going to be that day. Today, Cado was going to remain permanently glued to his father.

"When are you planning to go to the Bristol offices?" Will asked suddenly. "I think I know a couple of people over there who could develop some programmes for me to then check through. Maybe I could go over with you."

Lance shrugged his shoulders.

"I'm not going over today. Maybe I'll do that after the weekend, on Monday. I'm sure a couple of days won't hurt. We'll see how things are going then and make a fresh start."

Maybe they could all move forwards, have the staff involved and hopefully be more inclined to be on their side. Maybe this wasn't so bad after all. Life in fact seemed to be growing increasingly better as each day passed. Nothing could stop them now.

Chapter Thirty-Seven

Lance reluctantly got up off his chair. Rick and Will looked at him then checked their watches and said nothing. They knew where he would be going, and they could only guess how long it would be before he returned again. They didn't need to ask any questions.

Lance left the office and hurried over to the house. Gwyn was making a Christmas pudding while Cado sat in his high chair with two of his favourite toys to play with. The heady aroma of spices filled the air. Lance was unable to stop himself from smiling as he joined them. He ruffled Cado's hair and kissed Gwyn.

"I'm just off to the airport. Hopefully we'll not be long."

Gwyn smiled as she watched him disappear into the hall. He grabbed his coat and car keys and left the house through the front door. The atmosphere was damp and cold, the weather not really doing anything. There were no blue skies or clouds overhead. There was just a cold dampness in the air. They had endured this non-descript weather for days, and there was no imminent change in the forecast. They had been far too busy in the office to notice it though.

Lance climbed into his car and headed towards the airport. Large droplets of water formed by the moisture in the air occasionally fell to the ground. Some of them hit the car before ending on the road. The traffic grew increasingly heavier as he drove along the road. He at last parked at the airport and made his way into the terminal building. He could now only watch the arrivals board and wait for the flight from New York to arrive.

He helped his parents with their luggage and loaded the cases into the boot of his car before they climbed in. They had a lot of news to catch up on. Their workload had increased, despite the help they had from the office staff in Bristol. Will had found five people he trusted to tackle the development of the programmes, and he had put them to work immediately. They still seemed to have a mountain of work of their own each day, and the last few weeks in particular had been completely manic.

"Are you sure you want us to stay with you?" Nancy asked. "We could easily stay somewhere else instead, like the apartment in Bristol."

"I've sold it," Lance confessed. "We went over to check it after I'd got back from Boston. I didn't want it, not after Cindy had been there. It was an absolute tip and filthy. Gwyn didn't leave it like that when we moved out. She insisted on leaving it spotless. We hired in a house clearance firm and some professional cleaners then sold it. I really didn't want to keep anything associated with Cindy. Besides, Gwyn's expecting you to stay with us. She's got everything ready."

So the Bristol apartment, like Blake's Boston apartment and house in the hills, was gone too. Lance honestly wouldn't feel comfortable staying in any of the properties, and particularly the house. He couldn't go there, not after what Cindy and Phil had done there.

"Are you actually going to come back to Boston at some time?" Nancy asked.

"Yes, but I'm not going without Gwyn and Cado next time. Rick and Will are keen to see the Boston offices too. We'll probably stay in a hotel or something. I don't mind us visiting now I know it's safe for us to go there."

"It sounds as though you don't miss Boston."

Lance was quiet for a few moments. A lot had happened since he had first left Boston and came here. After all the turmoil, he felt calmest and safest when close to Avalon. That was here, and was safely tucked away in their wood at home. That was where he felt he belonged the most. His future had been decided in the first moment he had come across the mystical lake. He was fated to remain here with Gwyn. He was happiest when he was here.

"I don't really know Boston, mom. I was only allowed in the offices, the apartment or in the country house. I can't miss something I don't know anything about. I'll never feel settled or happy if I had to leave everything I have here and return to Boston."

Nancy looked more than a little disappointed. She had hoped that Lance had changed his mind since his last visit to America. She was still convinced that Boston was where he really belonged. She couldn't doubt his resolute determination to stay here though. She had to be content with the occasional visit. This wasn't the answer she wanted, but it was the answer she had to accept.

They arrived at the house and carried the suitcases to the guest bedroom. Gwyn had finished her baking and was now handing round mugs of coffee and home-made mince pies. They were in the living room, the lights already switched on despite it only being early afternoon. The other three were still working furiously in the office. Lance knew he should be with them, but he was loathed to leave Gwyn alone with his mother. He knew from past experience that Nancy would try to influence Gwyn instead. He could imagine his mother's attempt to convince his wife to move over to Boston.

Gwyn smiled quietly as she watched him reluctantly leave them. She could tell from his behaviour that something made him nervous. He would, in time, reveal all and tell her what was playing on his mind. He now had work to do and needed to return to the office. They were inundated with orders with Christmas fast approaching. Anna needed a hand. She was unable to keep up with the demand by herself.

The group looked round when the office door opened, despite being frantically busy. David stepped inside and hesitated warily while he closed the door. He was unsure of the greeting he would receive as he offered his help. He soon found himself in the middle of the action. They finally seemed to be making some headway, the afternoon all too quickly coming to a close. They closed down the computers and locked the office for the night. Lance and David then headed back to the house as Rick, Will and Anna drove away.

Lance opened the kitchen door as he thanked David and stepped back into the warmth of the house.

Gwyn was serving out dinner while Cado sat in his high chair with his meal already before him. Nancy poured out mugs of tea and put them beside the plates on the table. They at last sat down to a proper meal, with Gwyn and Lance sitting on one side of the table and Nancy and David on the other. The conversation was light and amiable as they focused upon Christmas. They couldn't deny it was fast approaching.

Cado was allowed to stay up for a while longer before he was settled in his cot. Gwyn waited until he had fallen asleep before she returned to the living room. Lance was talking to his parents, and he had just asked his mother how her shop was doing. He knew it was guaranteed to distract her from her incessant desire to move them to Boston.

"It's doing amazingly. I wish you'd come over and see for yourself. I've needed to take on extra staff to keep up with the demand. The designs are becoming really popular. They're appealing to more and more people right across America. I'm actually thinking about testing the water and make enquiries to see if it's worth me opening up more shops across America."

Lance stared at his mother and barely glanced at Gwyn as she sat beside him. Nancy sounded as though she was starting to take over. She was talking about Gwyn's designs. He looked stunned, while Gwyn was calm and relaxed.

"We discussed this while you were busy in the office. It's only a possibility at the moment. Nothing's certain yet. We need to do some research to see if it's financially viable. There's nothing you need to worry about. You've already got enough to think about without worrying about this too. We're not going to do anything rash. We know how to be sensible."

Lance gazed at her and relaxed a little. He couldn't say anything. It was Gwyn's business and her decision. His mother had at least actually sat down and discussed it with her. It was still very early days with no imminent decision being made. He really did have more than enough of his own to think about with his new empire. He was still trying to restructure the Bristol offices, and he was slowly beginning to make some progress. The manic rush before Christmas had put a stop to his plans and slowed him up. He was being forced to wait until Christmas and the New Year were over before he could continue on from where he was forced to temporarily stop.

He still had so much he needed to do. He preferred not to think about a lot of it. Pressure was increasing, however, and forcing him to face the fact that David was his biological father. His presence here now was bringing it one step closer. Maybe he should deal with this once and for all. Maybe he and David should go over to Avalon, where they could sit in peace and tranquillity while discussing how they really felt. Maybe tomorrow morning, while it was still fresh in his mind, they could sort this out so they could finally move on.

Chapter Thirty-Eight

Lance and David let themselves out of the house and quickly pulled the door shut behind them. The weather was still damp and overcast, and the plain white sky gave no colour to anything while miniscule droplets of moisture saturated the air. In contrast, it was warm and dry in the house. Gwyn and Nancy had been too wrapped up in the possible expansion of shops across America to notice them slip outside. They weren't heading to the office though. They were instead making their way to the wood.

The surrounding air suddenly felt warm and dry when they disappeared into the trees. They were sheltered in here from the depressing and non-descript weather that stubbornly refused to move on. In here, there was no weather. In here, there was just a constant calmness and tranquillity that soothed and cheered anyone who knew and understood the secret hidden in the trees. They were protected from the outside world in here, despite the lack of leaves on the overhead branches. They stepped onto the pale green grass that surrounded the lake, where the damp and dismal weather still couldn't penetrate the wood's defences.

The glowing white light was warm and welcoming as it reflected off the surface of the water. A ghostly haze covered the scene, with the swirling mist the only thing to move. David was mesmerised as he gazed at the island. He hesitated as Lance sat on the grass then joined him. This was where Lance came when he needed to think. It helped him unravel the tangle in his mind, and it helped him make sense of anything that bothered him. He wouldn't make sense of anything if he didn't have this sacred place to come to.

David suddenly felt compelled to speak after soaking up the atmosphere.

"Don't let your mom force you to give this place up, Lance. If you really want to live here, then don't feel obliged to move back over to Boston. She'll get over her disappointment, though she's already tried to talk Gwyn into moving to America."

"I know. I expected mom to try and convince her we should go. Gwyn's known for her diplomacy though, and she's given mom something else to think about instead."

David guessed he meant the possibility of opening a chain of stores and smiled.

"She's very enthusiastic. She's already talking about hundreds of stores right across America. I'm sure she'll become bored with it all before it's got out of control."

Lance smiled and hesitated before he spoke again.

"There's something we need to talk about. It's got nothing to do with work or the offices. I'm not saying it doesn't need discussing. There's still lots that needs sorting out. There's something we've been avoiding, and it's not going to go away. We haven't talked about you actually being my real father."

They both felt nervous and tense as Lance continued.

"I don't blame you for what happened. I don't blame any of you. I can even understand and accept why you did it. I only wish I'd been told sooner. I wish I'd always known."

They both quickly looked round. Blake Brookes had finally agreed to come and speak to him. Lance scrambled up onto his feet as Blake spoke.

"I'm the one to blame. I refused to let them tell you anything. They'd given me the son I was desperate for. They'd given me you, and I didn't want them to take you away from me. I didn't want you to want to be with them more. I chased your mom away from you and insisted you were raised by someone I chose. I was scared you'd turn against me. I thought if I moulded you into the person I wanted you to be then you'd not turn your back on me. It was too late when I realised how wrong I was. I bullied you all. I forced my wishes on you all and refused to listen."

Blake paused a moment, but not for long enough to give Lance or David the chance to say anything. He continued on, and he was still not prepared to listen to anyone else.

"Your mom wanted you to know about David from the very start. She wanted you to grow up knowing exactly what we'd done and why we'd done it. I didn't let her though. I forced her away and denied you your mother for most of your life instead. Nancy and David have done nothing wrong."

Lance gazed at him for a few moments then stared into space. David had stood up, and he now stood beside Lance. He couldn't understand this. Blake Brookes was dead. He had attended his funeral and watched as he had been buried. This surely couldn't be possible. How could it be that Blake was now standing here in front of them? Blake was now looking directly at David.

"You're a good man," he said. "It was wrong of me to refuse to let you play any part in Lance's upbringing. You could've taught him so much. He's so much like you. He's inherited your talent. I nearly ruined all of that with my methods and behaviour. You're going to make an awesome and unbeatable team."

"You could've been a part of this too," Lance told him.

Blake shook his head.

"Don't kid yourself, Lance. It would've never happened. I'd have never listened to you. I would've stubbornly refused to change my ways, and you know that. I'd have carried on in my usual brutish way. I'd have continued to bully and intimidate you so you wouldn't show everyone how useless I really was. I'd have taken everything Cindy did to me out on you. I'd have blamed you for what happened to me. I'd have never admitted or accepted responsibility for my own actions, even if I did have the courage to face everyone again. You can't deny I'm just a bully and a coward."

"No, you've achieved so much," Lance objected.

"I achieved nothing, Lance. I only ever used other people then claimed all the glory for myself. I thought nothing of bleeding people dry then tossing them aside. I had to pass over, an act made easier with Guinevere's help. I'd have continued to force my views on everyone while picking fault with you. What you're doing with my company is already proving to be an improvement. I'd have refused to implement any of your changes. I'd have stubbornly carried on in my own way instead. I'd have believed I knew better. I'd have never listened to you. I was no good to you. It's time for you to live your life in the way you want to live it."

Blake still refused to let Lance speak. He was the one who had always spoken while everyone else was expected to listen. Lance had every right to be angry with him. He had made his life a living hell. He needed to now close that chapter of his life. He needed to turn his back on Blake and embrace his parents. They had so much to offer him. They could achieve so much more together. Blake had done nothing for him except give him a lifetime of misery. Arthur and Guinevere had rescued him from his tyranny. They had helped him escape, though Blake had still needed to pass over to free him properly. He wasn't worth any more consideration. Lance needed to let David be the father he always wanted to be. It was time for him to show the world what a formidable force he was.

Blake refused to listen to Lance any more. He had said what he wanted to say. He didn't want to be asked any awkward questions. He had shouldered all the blame and accepted responsibility for everything that had happened. He moved back and hovered above the surface of the lake for a brief moment. He then slowly faded away. The mist continued to glow in the white light as peace and tranquillity once again descended upon the scene.

David was confused and unnerved by what he had just witnessed. He couldn't think of anything to say as an awkward silence reigned for a few long and agonising moments. The apparition that had stood before them had spoken the truth. David eventually found his voice.

"I can't deny I was forced to be shut out of your life, Lance," he blurted out. "Marrying your mom opened the door and let me in. I knew I had to still keep the secret. I really wanted you to like me, even if I did have to masquerade as your step-father. The truth's out now though, and I really hope you can forgive us."

Lance remained quiet for a while.

"My… Blake's right about not listening. He would've realised we were about to discuss where we go from here if he had."

"Where would you like us to go to?" David asked.

Lance glanced at him then fixed his gaze on the grass in front of him.

"I don't know. I do know I'd like to find out what it's like to have a proper relationship with you. I've felt cheated, but I don't want to live my life like I'd been expected to. You've given me a lot of support in the last year, and I feel closer to you because of it. I know it's going to be difficult and awkward at first, and the hardest thing for me to do is call you 'dad'. I've never called anyone 'dad'. I've only ever called… him 'sir'. If you don't mind, I'd like to start calling you that."

David smiled and gave Lance a quick hug.

"That's something I'd like very much."

The tension inside Lance began to drain away as he managed a smile. He had taken the first step. He had begun to open up a little and accept David into his life.

"Do you want us to move over to Boston?" he asked.

"Move you away from this? I couldn't make you leave all this if you don't want to."

"We wouldn't be," Lance confessed. "It'd follow us and be wherever we live. I think it belongs here though. I can't see it surviving in Boston itself. Besides, I'd only be reminded of what my life used to be like if I lived there. I'm happy living here, and I can't see that changing."

"Well don't tell your mom that. She'll have you moving back in a flash if she did. If you want to stay here, then I'll respect that. Besides, it'd be an excuse for me to come over and see where I come from. I was born in a village near here."

"Thanks, dad."

The two words came out naturally as Lance realised he did have the local connection he had needed to free King Arthur after all. The revelation had caught him by surprise and made his heart thump. He now looked embarrassed as he realised what he had said. The moment passed as David smiled and hugged him again.

It was time to return to the modern world and face the other issues that still needed discussing. The taboo subject of the true identity of Lance's biological father was broached and overcome. Maybe they could now begin to move on.

Chapter Thirty-Nine

Gwyn smiled quietly while she sat beside Lance on one of the two settees. Cado was surrounded by new toys and brightly coloured packaging as he sat on the floor. He wasn't complaining about all his gifts, despite having no idea what this was all about. The television was switched on but playing to no one. It simply provided some background noise. No one was really interested in it.

Dinner was cooking in the kitchen, and the aroma of roasting turkey filled the house. Nancy and David were sitting on the other settee. They all knew Gwyn would slip out of the room in a few minutes to serve out dinner. The morning had passed so quickly, with Cado the centre of attention. The past few weeks had been so incredibly hectic. Lance was now getting the chance to relax.

Gwyn stood up and quietly disappeared out of the room. Cado watched her go, but quickly decided to remain where he was. He was comfortable while in the company of his father and grandparents, and he was too preoccupied with his new toys to worry about his mother's disappearance. She made her way to the kitchen and began to serve out Christmas dinner. She preferred to complete this task on her own instead of working around others. She guessed they would still be talking, though any talk of work was banned today.

Gwyn gazed out of the kitchen window. Her mind was miles away. She didn't see the damp and dismal weather that still tightly gripped the area. She was used to this type of weather at this time of year. It didn't bother her at all. The house was warm and dry, and everyone was happy. She smiled as she continued to serve out the food onto the plates. Lance and David were getting on with each other more as each day passed. Since their visit to Avalon, their relationship in fact had improved immensely. Lance was helped enormously by Blake's appearance and the words he said. He had moved on at last.

Gwyn could only guess the courage Blake needed to muster to face Lance, especially while having David by his side. He had shouldered all the blame and accepted responsibility for everything that had gone so badly wrong. David had been unnerved by the apparition before him and Lance. Lance had needed another two days to finally accept what had been said to him, and now that David had recovered from his shock, they had begun to bond.

Talk had inevitably moved to the company. They didn't want to confuse anyone, so they decided to leave the company name unchanged. They were now working towards moulding the company to run it in the way they wanted. The man employed to manage the Bristol offices had joined them and joined in with the initial discussions of what they planned to do. The group had made arrangements to meet in the Bristol offices to begin implementing the changes they wanted to make once the New Year was over.

Gwyn and Nancy had continued to discuss their own plans with the men out of the way without fear of interruptions or meddling. Gwyn, in truth, liked the idea of a chain of stores right across America. There was no denying it was an ambitious plan, though she couldn't quite understand why Nancy refused to agree to let other craft shops stock their designs. Nancy seemed to want complete control and exclusivity. They only planned to open two more stores at first, with one on Florida and the other in California. They wanted to see how well they did before they decided whether to close them or open more. That was in the future though. That was something to work on and look forward to. Nancy's enthusiasm was addictive, Gwyn wasn't denying that. Now though she was supposed to be serving out their Christmas dinner.

Gwyn called the others and put the last of the plates on the table as they joined her. Lance sat Cado in his high chair then sat beside Gwyn while David opened a bottle of wine. Gwyn looked round at everyone and smiled quietly again. She had her family with her. Gareth had disowned her and forged a comfortable new life for himself in Thailand. This was her new life. She had her family around her and a life destined to get even better.

David proposed a toast to the future. She echoed his words and took a sip from her glass. To the future, and all the excitement it would bring. That was a whole new chapter in their lives though. Blake had passed over and left the way clear for them to mould the future in the way they wanted. Nothing would be the same again without Blake around. Gwyn said nothing as she listened to the conversation being held around the table. At the same time, ideas for new designs for her to work on were forming in her mind. Christmas or not, she needed to pull out her pencil and paper once dinner was eaten. Life was going to be far more relaxed with Blake gone. It was time to close that chapter and look forwards. She could do that, and Lance seemed ready to do that too. David's simple toast had said it all. They could embark on a new beginning and leave the past behind.

A feeble and watery sun suddenly pierced through the nondescript mist. It shone through the window and provided a little more light. Gwyn looked round and silently acknowledged what it symbolised. The future was beginning right now, and it was looking brighter. They had the world at their feet, and they were being rewarded for their belief and loyalty. Nothing could get in their way or stop them. They belonged together. They were the new formidable force, and one that would always remember what true friendship was. A peaceful calm had descended upon them, so each of them felt truly and completely contented. Gwyn smiled at Cado and continued to eat her meal. The new chapter was beginning, and they were ready and willing to embrace it. It was time to let this new chapter begin.

THE END

Lightning Source UK Ltd.
Milton Keynes UK
UKHW02f0349140918
328845UK00003B/27/P